TWO WEEK DEAL

A STRUCK BY LOVE NOVEL

SYRIE JAMES

This book is a work of fiction. Names, characters, places, organizations, incidents, and dialogue are drawn from the the author's imagination and are not to be construed as real. Any resemblance to actual events or persons, living or dead, is entirely coincidental.

TWO WEEK DEAL

Previously published as *Propositions* and *The Sky's The Limit.*

NOCTURNE
    "Lyrical, lush, and intensely romantic." —*Library Journal*

THE SECRET DIARIES OF CHARLOTTE BRONTË
    Audiobook Audie Award for Romance
    "Syrie James takes the biography of Brontë and sketches it into a work of art." —*Sacramento Book Review*

THE LOST MEMOIRS OF JANE AUSTEN
    "The reader pulls for the heroine and her dreams of love ... offers a deeper understanding of what Austen's life might have been like." —*The Los Angeles Times*

DRACULA, MY LOVE
    "A spooky yet thoroughly romantic love story." —*Chicago Tribune*

THE MISSING MANUSCRIPT OF JANE AUSTEN
    "A literary feast for Anglophiles." —*Publishers Weekly*

    "This richly imagined Jane Austen 'road novel' is such a page turner!"—*Kirkus Reviews* (starred review)

FORBIDDEN
    "If you enjoy angels, 'forbidden' romance and dashing heroes, this should be added to your TBR." —*USA Today*

JANE AUSTEN'S FIRST LOVE
    "Truly riveting. James's latest will charm Austen fans as well as Austen unfamiliars ... Romance fans will root for Jane all the way." —*Library Journal*, Editor's Pick

CHAPTER 1

South Lake Tahoe, California
December 1987

The slot machine whirred. Three bright streaks of red, blue, and orange whizzed past. Kelli took a sharp breath and held it, watching as the first cylinder dropped into place with a clang: an orange on the top row, a plum in the center, cherries below. Three chances to win.

A split second later came another clang. Another plum in the center. The third cylinder continued its mad spin. Could it be? Another plum? Three plums and she'd win—

A cluster of red cherries popped into the slot next to the plums. The slot machine froze into metallic stillness.

Kelli sighed. No wonder they called it a one-armed bandit. In five seconds, she'd lost a third of tomorrow's lunch money.

Oh well, she thought with a shrug. *Fortunes like mine come and go.* She didn't drive all the way from Seattle to South Lake Tahoe to gamble, anyway.

She came to watch over her brother Kyle's vacation home in its last three weeks of construction and to get in some skiing—a few days of glorious downhill on some of Lake Tahoe's finest slopes. And of course, there was the job interview in San Francisco.

Kelli slid up onto the stool next to the slot machine and straightened the calf-length skirt of her white silk evening dress. *Last summer,* she thought with amusement, *if someone had told her she'd be sitting in a casino lobby on a Friday night in early December, waiting for a man she barely knew—a man who might be her next employer—to escort her to an exclusive holiday mixer on the hotel's top floor, she wouldn't have believed it.*

If she hadn't acted so impulsively, hadn't let her temper get the best of her, she'd still be working away at the ad agency in Seattle. But in the past year she'd experienced a rash of compulsions to do the boldest, most brazen things. Like the time she accepted Kyle's dare and took over the controls of his twin-engine Bonanza over Puget Sound. *Crazy!*

And the morning, six months ago, when she asked Wayne to pack up his things and move out, then told her boss of four years to go fly a kite and stormed out the office door without a backward glance. *Madness!* Her actions had shocked everyone. Including herself.

It was only later, in the ensuing weeks on her own, that she'd come to understand her motivation. For twenty-eight years she'd allowed well-meaning parents and sisters and then a domineering boyfriend to influence her every move.

Afraid of losing her job, she'd kept silent while higher-ups stole her best design work and claimed it as their own. All the while her resentment had simmered, until finally she'd blown her stack.

Life, she'd come to realize—like the ad slogan she'd helped to create—is *not* a spectator sport. Never again would she calmly sit back, letting people manipulate and take advantage of her. She was going to be in the driver's seat from now on.

She hadn't wasted any time getting her new life in order. Out from under Wayne's judgmental eye, she felt more capable, more attractive.

She had a slender figure, a face that men seemed to notice, and stick-straight reddish-brown hair that her hairdresser envied. The world was overflowing with limitless, exciting possibilities, and she was going to enjoy every minute of it.

She had immediately indulged herself in all the things Wayne would have disapproved of. She bought clothes that were beautiful, not practical, ate take-out Chinese food five nights in a row, and went to see movies *she* liked—all comedies and romances without a single too-macho hero or blast of machine-gun fire.

She'd felt terrific, like a new woman, like a caged sparrow at last set free.

She'd decided not to work for another advertising agency and tried freelancing instead. Within a few months she'd built up a small but steady clientele and was enjoying herself immensely. She loved being her own boss, reporting to no one, allowing her creative energies to have free reign.

The only problem was money. Business was undependable—too busy one week and quiet the next.

When Bob Dawson called from San Francisco, he'd caught her in a weak moment. She'd just gone over her bank statement. She'd been forced to admit that her earnings barely covered her living expenses, and her savings would be gone in another month.

Bob had seen her design work on a recent, award-winning campaign, and had tracked her down. He'd been so profuse with his compliments that when he asked her to come down for an interview, she couldn't say no.

She had to be in South Lake Tahoe for three weeks anyway, to watch over her brother's house. So she'd agreed to stop off in the city to meet Bob at his office on the way.

"Your artwork and design show remarkable versatility," Bob had said at their meeting two days earlier. "I've been looking for someone like you to take over when our creative director leaves next month. We've got an exciting campaign coming up for Cassera's Hotel and Casino, one of our largest accounts, and I'd like you to work on it."

She'd been amazed by the generous salary he'd offered —even more amazed when he'd invited her to the party tonight to meet Ted Lazar, the casino's general manager. It was an excellent professional opportunity, the dream position that she'd been working toward for six long years.

She hadn't liked Bob at first, although she couldn't say why—and then she'd decided she was wrong. He turned out to be polite and charming. She ought to have accepted the job in a flash. Instead, she'd told him she needed time to think it over.

Why was she hesitating?

People in jeans and ski jackets streamed in through the double glass doors at the casino's nearby side entrance, bringing in laughter, a blast of cold air, and a flurry of snowflakes. Kelli checked her watch again. Nine o'clock.

Bob was an hour late. What could be keeping him? What if he never showed up?

This is ridiculous, Kelli decided. Go on up to the party and let him join you.

She slid off the stool and hurried past the slot-machine area, around the corner to the hotel elevators. A bell announced the impending arrival of the closest elevator and she stopped in front of it. The doors hissed open and she took a purposeful step forward.

At the same instant a man propelled himself out, and they collided with an impact that sent Kelli staggering backward. She uttered a startled cry just as hands grabbed her arms to steady her, and she found herself eye to eye with the lapel of a charcoal-grey suit.

"Excuse me," said a deep voice.

He took a step sideways, away from the elevator and the other departing passengers. She looked up, still numb with surprise, into a face that was handsome even though its dark brows were drawn together in a distracted scowl.

He looked a few years older than she was. Thirty, maybe thirty-two. He had a straight nose, a determined set to his jaw, and a wide mouth that was pressed together in a tight line. His short, dark brown hair gleamed beneath the overhead lights.

The survey took only a fraction of an instant. He stood just inches away, still gripping her arms with his head tilted down to hers, so that despite his height, she couldn't help but stare directly into his eyes. They were a rich, vibrant blue, like the Tahoe sky, surrounded by thick, dark lashes; quick, intelligent eyes, which at this moment sparked with irritation.

Despite this—for some inexplicable reason—she felt a sudden, wild fluttering inside her—a feeling of momentous, impending change.

"Fate," she thought, and realized, too late, that she'd said it out loud.

He released her arms. His scowl vanished and his eyes lit with interest and a surprising warmth. "What?"

She cleared her throat. "Nothing."

"I thought you said fate."

"No, I said ... late."

"Late?"

"I'm ... late," she said. "For a very important ... date."

His lips twitched with amusement. "Curiouser and curiouser."

She realized she'd babbled a line straight out of *Alice's Adventures in Wonderland,* and he'd responded in kind. She blushed.

"I'm sorry I rammed into you. I shouldn't have been in such a hurry."

"My fault." He waved away her apology. "I wasn't in the world's best mood, or I would have watched where—" In a single, rapid glance he took in her formal attire, and a speculative gleam came into his eyes. "You wouldn't by any chance be going to the party upstairs, would you? The one on the top floor?"

"Yes, I am."

"And you're on the list? They're expecting you?"

"I think so."

He rubbed his chin thoughtfully for a moment. "Listen, would you ... " He checked his watch and a perturbed look flitted across his face.

"I know this is an imposition, but can I ask you a favor? I'm supposed to meet someone at that party, but it looks like he forgot to leave my name at the door. No one gets in if they're not on the list, and they've got Attila the Hun guarding the door. I've come up all the way from San Francisco and I'll be damned if I'm going to leave now."

"So, you want me to ... what?" Kelli asked, a spark of excitement surging through her. "Smuggle you in? Pretend you're my date?"

He nodded, his eyes searching her face. "Would you?"

"I don't know. Who are you supposed to meet?"

"Ted Lazar."

"The casino general manager?" The very man Bob wanted her to meet tonight.

He nodded.

"What's it about?"

"Business." He waved his hand impatiently. "It's too complicated to go into. But the timing on this thing is critical, and it's getting late. I want to get in there before Ted decides to take off."

Kelli wondered how much of his story was true. *Business*, he'd said. How vague was that? What if he was using her to get inside for some illicit purpose? No, she couldn't believe that. She saw no threat in his anxious, blue gaze.

Instinct told her she could trust him. And the element of intrigue ... well, intrigued her.

The elevator touched down again and a handful of people in party dress spewed out. "Well?" he asked, gesturing toward the waiting lift.

Life is not a spectator sport, Kelli reminded herself. This was the most interesting, attractive man she'd met in years. A smile lit her face.

"Sure. Why not?" She stepped lightly into the empty elevator in front of him.

He punched the button for the top floor. "I can't tell you how much I appreciate this." They began to ascend, and he leaned against the side wall and smiled at her for the first time. He looked even more handsome when he smiled. Disarmingly so.

"What's your name?"

"Kelli Ann Harrison."

"Kelli Ann. Beautiful name. It suits you."

She held on to the side rail, her heart beating oddly as his eyes held hers for a long moment. "Thanks. And you are?"

"Grant Pembroke."

"Hi, Grant."

He said hi back, his gaze never leaving her face. Bemused by his intense study, she dragged her eyes away from his, focusing instead on the collar of his expensive-looking blue shirt.

His suit was beautifully tailored and looked expensive, too. He probably had a desk job. No, something more adventuresome than that. "Are you with the CIA?"

His eyes widened. "The CIA?"

"Well, you know, all this cloak-and-dagger stuff. Very suspicious."

He laughed. It was a low-pitched, pleasant laugh, and she liked the way it sounded in the enclosed space. "This is hardly cloak and dagger. More like block and tackle."

She wanted to ask him more, but the elevator slowed and jerked to a halt. Another bevy of partygoers waited in the hotel hallway as they squeezed out.

Grant led the way down the ribbon of red-and-black patterned carpet to a small table where a stocky guard in the hotel uniform sat reading a magazine. Kelli could hear the hum of laughter and conversation through the closed door beside him marked Presidential Suite.

"My date finally got here." Grant told the guard Kelli's name. "Check and see if Lazar put her on the list instead of me."

The doorman picked up a sheaf of papers from the table and made a slow, meticulous check mark beside her name.

"This man is with you?" he asked, frowning.

Kelli smiled and nodded. With a shrug, he hauled himself out of his chair and opened the door. Grant accompanied her inside, where a crowd of people in elegant evening dress milled against a backdrop of soft music and drifting cigarette smoke.

Christmas was still three weeks away, but the room, like the rest of the hotel and casino, was alive with tasteful holiday décor. Tantalizing aromas wafted toward her from an elaborate hors d'oeuvres table in the center of the room.

Grant drew her away from the door and leaned close to her ear. "Thanks," he whispered.

His breath was a sweet, moist vapor against skin that seared with unexpected heat.

"You're welcome," she said softly.

He straightened and inclined his head to search through the crowd. His hand still at her back, he said distractedly, "Will you be free later? Because if you are, this won't take long. Would you like to meet back here in say, about an hour?"

Kelli was seized by an impulse to accept, to say as a matter of fact, I'm free for the evening, and I'd love to meet you anywhere, anytime. But reason intervened. Bob *had* invited her, and he'd show up any minute.

"I'm sorry. I can't. I'm meeting someone."

Grant's blue eyes dimmed with apparent regret. "Anyone important?"

"Possibly my boss."

"Possibly your boss?"

"He offered me a position with his company. I haven't accepted it yet."

"I see." He ran a hand through his hair and shook his head with a worried frown. "Still, is this going to get you in trouble? Letting me in like that? The doorman's sure to tell him—"

"Don't worry about it. I'll come up with some excuse."

"I don't know. I'd hate to see—"

"I'll be fine. Honest."

He sighed. "Well, then, so be it." He paused for a couple of heartbeats, looking into her eyes. "Goodbye, Kelli Ann Harrison." He held out his hand.

She placed her hand in his. As she returned his firm

handshake, unsteady pulses began to thump in strange places in her body.

"Thanks again," he said.

She had to blink twice to watch him as he turned and wove his way through the crowd. It wasn't until he'd disappeared from sight that she let out the breath she'd been holding in a long, wistful sigh.

Well. So much for a brush with destiny—the proverbial chance encounter with a mysterious stranger. She had acted spontaneously, lived a bit dangerously, then duty called and poof! She was right back where she started.

Normal, everyday existence.

She caught herself. What was wrong with normal? Things were shaping up very nicely in her life at the moment, thank you very much. She relished her independence. She wasn't looking for another entangling relationship. She'd barely recovered from the last one. It was just as well that Grant had walked away.

Kelli wandered idly through the room for several minutes, observing the partygoers, mulling over a few possible explanations to give Bob. A tuxedoed waiter offered her a glass of champagne—one of her favorite beverages—but she declined, wanting to keep her head clear for the meeting to come.

Instead, she crossed to the circular buffet table, where a tiered silver centerpiece spilled over with fresh fruit of every color and description. An attractive arrangement of trays below was filled with plump prawns, stuffed mushrooms, puff pastries, and marinated chicken wings. The mingling aromas made her mouth water.

She was about to reach for a plate when a laugh caught

her attention. Her eyes shot toward an adjoining room, where among the milling crowd, she saw Grant shaking hands with a rotund man in a dark-blue suit. Lazar? she wondered hopefully.

A giddy sense of elation swept over her, as if she'd just helped perpetrate an undercover scheme of vast magnitude and importance. He couldn't have done it without me, she thought—and then realized she didn't know what *it* was.

Was that fair? Couldn't he at least have told her what business he was in?

She slipped into the next room, squeezed between a knot of people, and stopped behind a leafy potted palm as tall as the door.

I'll just listen long enough to find out why he's here, she promised herself, parting the fronds slightly and peering through at Grant's back a few feet away.

"Don't be too hard on him, Ted," Grant was saying. *Ted. So, it was Ted Lazar.* "He was just doing his job."

"Job, shmob. I'm gonna give him hell." Ted was a head shorter than Grant, about the same height as herself, a paternal type with a fringe of white hair and a congenial yet commanding air. "Stupid of me to forget, it's been a hectic day, but he shouldn't have turned you away without looking for me."

"Don't worry about it," Grant said. "I managed to get in." Kelli liked the way his tapered grey suit jacket fit smoothly across the wide expanse of his shoulders and the slope of his back. "I know you're on a tight deadline, so I didn't want to waste any time. I've had my eye on Cassera's for years, Ted. We're the people you're looking for. We can do a hell of a job for you."

"Not so fast, Grant." Ted's laugh was low and gravelly. "I didn't promise anything. I just said we'd talk."

"If you're not happy with the people handling you now, I'd think you'd want to do more than just talk."

"Maybe." Ted lifted a cigar to his lips and inhaled deeply, then squinted puffy eyes and blew out a slow column of smoke. "When you called this morning, I agreed to meet you because I've seen your work. Damned good. One of the best ad agencies in San Francisco, I'm told, even if you're not one of the biggest. And your list of clients is impressive."

Kelli let the palm fronds flip back into place and froze, her heart pounding in sudden comprehension. Grant Pembroke owned an advertising agency. He was here to try to steal the casino account from Bob Dawson!

"Kelli! There you are." A hand touched Kelli's shoulder and she jumped, repressing a startled scream. "I've been looking all over for you," Bob said.

He wore a black suit and striped shirt that looked positively dapper, and his thick silvery-blond mane was carefully combed, not a hair out of place.

"Sorry I'm so late," he continued. "I got tied up at the office and couldn't get away. Then traffic was horrendous —it took me five hours to get here." He elbowed his way back into the main suite, pulling her with him. "The guard told me you came in with someone. Why didn't you tell me you wanted to bring a friend?"

"I ran into him unexpectedly," Kelli said. That was certainly true, wasn't it? "He only stayed a few minutes."

"Where did he go? You shouldn't have brought him up here. He wasn't cleared." Bob grabbed two champagne glasses from a passing tray and handed one to Kelli. He raised his glass. "To my newest and most attractive creative director. Cheers." He took a long drink.

I haven't accepted the job yet, Kelli wanted to tell him, staring dubiously at her glass. Champagne was for celebrations. Weddings. Christenings. Bon-voyage parties. Romantic evenings for two. Somehow, she didn't feel like celebrating tonight.

"What do you think about all this?" Bob indicated the crowded room with a nod of his head. "Did you take a look around the casino? Ever work on an account this size?" He took another drink. "Wait till you meet Lazar. He's a sweetheart of a guy. Let's go find him and introduce you."

Kelli tensed with anxiety. "No, wait." Grant would no doubt be talking to Ted Lazar for a while. What would Bob say if he discovered she'd admitted one of his competitors to the party? Somehow, she had to keep them apart.

"Before I meet him I should know everything that's going on with the account," she said, trying to stall for time. "You told me yesterday there's a big campaign coming up?"

Bob nodded. "*Big* is an understatement. The board decided they're tired of the old logo and the look we've been using on all the collateral materials. They want a brand-new print image for the hotel and casino, everything revamped. And a new campaign to go with it."

Kelli took a surprised breath. Everything revamped. A hotel and casino this large would use a ton of collateral materials—brochures, menus, coupons, stationery, rate cards—not to mention a whole new ad campaign.

"The account's kept us pretty busy for six years. But we're talking big bucks now."

Kelli felt a rush of excitement. She'd never worked on a project of such magnitude. Dawson Advertising must not be on retainer, or Grant wouldn't be here trying to steal the account away. "Is anyone else bidding on this?"

"Just one agency, a small fish out of Reno. Routine stuff, to make sure our prices stay in line. Nothing to worry about."

So, he didn't know about Grant. "Why nothing to worry about?"

"They don't have a chance in hell of coming up with a workable campaign," Bob said with a self-indulgent smirk. "I took a little trip to Reno a few weeks ago. Three of the guy's top people are working for me now—his head account exec, copy chief, and art director. Wasn't hard to spirit them away. Even dedicated souls will move on if you offer them the right price."

His chuckle stopped when he saw the expression on her face. "Don't look so shocked. Everyone does it. It's a cutthroat business. You don't stay on top by sitting back and twiddling your thumbs. You've got to nip trouble in the bud before it starts."

Kelli didn't like where this was heading. Before she could reply, Bob drained his glass and went on:

"Take today, for instance. This hot shot from San Francisco tried to move in on my territory. When Ted told me that he'd called—Ted likes to keep me on my toes, it's a power trip he plays—hell, this account's been mine for six years. I'm not going to waste my time on a proposal of this size while he puts it out to bid to every Tom, Dick, and

Harry that comes along. And I'm sure as hell not going to let Pembroke Advertising steal it away."

Kelli's pulse quickened. "What did you do?"

"Just told Ted a few things I 'heard' about Pembroke." Bob chuckled. "Spread a few rumors."

"What did you say?" Kelli asked, her stomach knotting.

"Who cares, as long as it works? Fifty bucks says Ted won't give Grant Pembroke the time of day now."

Kelli felt sick. She'd been uncomfortable in Bob's office the day before, and now she knew why. This man's business tactics turned sleaze into a new art form. How could she have even considered working for him? How could she have considered working for *anyone*?

I may not make much money freelancing, she thought, but at least I have my integrity. She'd only agreed to the interview in a moment of financial despair.

Now she realized she'd never wanted the job in the first place. When she got back to Seattle, she'd build up her business, make a go of it somehow. And she'd never—no, *never*—work for anyone else again.

A weight seemed to lift from her shoulders with this decision, and her gaze slanted back into the adjoining room.

She spotted Grant, still talking to Ted Lazar. Did Grant know Bob was bad-mouthing him behind his back? Someone ought to tell him. She wondered if Ted believed the rumors about Grant, and whether they might ruin Grant's chances to bid on the account.

It would serve Bob right if Grant stole the account out from under his nose, she thought.

"Bob," she said, taking his arm and leading him deeper

into the crowd, away from Grant, "I wonder if you'd excuse me for a minute." She glanced meaningfully toward the front door and he nodded in understanding.

"The ladies' lounge is just down the hall," he said, pointing. "Look for me around here when you're through."

"I will." When he'd gone, Kelli made her way back through the crowd into the other room, her heart racing with anticipation. She stopped behind the palm plant again, listening.

"I appreciate you coming up here," Ted said. "The thing is, I don't want to waste your time on this if we're not right for each other. Why don't you call me next week? Give me a few days to check some things out before I give you any details."

"Check what out? Ted, I'll need to get started on this as soon as possible. Let's go down to your office, where it's quiet. Five minutes, that's all I ask."

Ted sighed. "Grant, let me be frank with you. I've heard nothing but praise for the work you do. But quality isn't the only thing I'm looking for. I need performance, someone who can meet my schedule, who's easy to work with. And since I talked to you last, I've heard a few things I don't like. Things that say you don't fit the bill."

"I don't fit the—what are you talking about? Who've you been talking to?"

"I heard you're temperamental," Ted said. "Stubborn. No one wants to work for you. You like to run the whole show. And worse yet, I hear you're slow. You take forever to finish a job."

"That's absurd. I probably have less staff turnover than any agency in the city. We meet our deadlines, Ted, and then some. Ask any one of my clients. I'll give you a list. You can call them tomorrow."

Kelli fumed inwardly. Bob Dawson's nasty rumors were working far too well. She had to do something to help.

Something ....

"I'll make a few calls tomorrow," Ted said. "Maybe I'll talk to someone who'll change my mind. But right now, I don't want to spend any more—"

"Excuse me." Kelli boldly moved forward and stopped at Grant's side. Out of the corner of her eye, she could see him stiffen in surprise. "Don't believe everything you've heard about Grant's temperament." She fixed Lazar with a dazzling smile. "He's not difficult to work with, I promise you. Honestly, he's a pussycat at heart. And as for the company being slow? Ridiculous. Ten minutes in your office and I'll prove otherwise."

Lazar's bushy brows lifted in fatherly admiration. "Is that right? And who are you, little lady?"

Kelli grinned at Grant, who was staring at her in wide-eyed astonishment, then turned back to Lazar and extended her hand. "I'm Kelli Ann Harrison, Creative Director for Pembroke Advertising."

CHAPTER 2

"Creative Director?" Ted Lazar beamed and shook Kelli's hand with a hearty grip.

His leathery face and kind, dark eyes reminded her of her feisty grandfather, and she liked him at once. "Grant, why didn't you introduce this lovely lady before? Where've you been hiding her?"

"I just arrived," Kelli said. "In fact, Grant wasn't even sure I'd be here tonight."

She heard a small choke from Grant beside her but plunged on. "But as long as I am, I thought, why not stop by and put in my two cents' worth?" She smiled brightly.

"Glad you did." Ted waved his cigar from Kelli to Grant and back again. "How long have you two been working together?"

"Not long," Grant said sharply.

Kelli dared a glance at Grant. His direct gaze seemed to pierce through her. The initial astonishment was gone, replaced by wary incomprehension and a silent, deadly serious warning.

She could only guess how all this would appear to him. He didn't know what she did for a living, didn't know she was only doing this to help him win the account. But there was no way to explain.

She'd gone this far; she couldn't back out now.

"I may be new with the company," Kelli told Ted, "but I can tell you this: any rumors you've heard about Grant's temperament are just that. Rumors. In all the time I've been with Grant, I've never heard him raise his voice to an employee or make an unreasonable demand of anyone."

And that, she thought, is the truth.

An even more puzzled look flashed across the deep blue of Grant's eyes. He opened his mouth to speak, then shut it again.

"Well, well, well. This puts a different light on things." The tip of Ted's cigar glowed as he inhaled deeply, then blew out a slow column of smoke. "Grant, if I'd known you had a charming associate who thinks so highly of you—" He shrugged. "I guess I can spare a few minutes in my office, as long as you're both here. Come with me."

"Hold on a minute, Ted," Grant said, but apparently Ted didn't hear.

Ted took Kelli's arm and led her away, through the crowd and out a nearby side door, commenting that the champagne hadn't been cold enough and anyway the line for the cocktail show would be starting soon downstairs and people would be leaving in droves.

Over her shoulder, Kelli saw Grant just a step or two behind.

"In here." Ted unlocked a wide door at the end of the hall and ushered them inside.

The large corner office was carpeted in deep, vivid blue and furnished in polished oak. Paneled walls were hung with oil paintings depicting Lake Tahoe's Mount Tallac in different seasons. There was a wet bar, an assortment of bonsai pine trees, and a row of what looked like antique slot machines.

But the most astonishing feature of the room was the view.

Kelli felt herself drawn to the solid wall of plate-glass windows across the back of the room. Stars twinkled in the inky darkness like finely cut diamonds, and the three-quarter moon cast a midnight-blue sheen on the waters of Lake Tahoe stretching out endlessly some fifteen stories below.

"Beautiful," Kelli said.

"You should see it by day." Ted moved around his desk, which was wider than a door and covered with a collection of bronze and glass figurines in athletic poses: snow skiing, golfing, sailing, waterskiing. From a credenza behind he picked up a stack of art boards covered in heavy blue paper.

"Miss Harrison—it is Miss, isn't it?"

"Yes. But please, call me Kelli."

Ted sat down in his large armchair, indicating the two leather chairs opposite the desk. "Take a seat. I don't have much time." He slid the stack of boards across a clear space of desk to rest in front of Kelli.

"Kelli, I'd like your opinion on this. It's a presentation our agency put together for us some weeks ago, for a series of—"

"We'd both be delighted to take a look at what you've

got," Grant cut in tersely, leaning a hand on the desk, "but if you want an off-the-cuff analysis, you'll have to get it from me."

"I'm familiar with your work, Pembroke." Ted motioned politely for Grant to move out of the way. "I want to hear what Kelli has to say."

"No!" Grant shook his head. "Look, Ted, Kelli doesn't—"

"What are you afraid of, Grant?" Ted glared at him. "Maybe those rumors are true, after all. Don't you have any faith in your employees? Do you always have to run the whole show? Let the woman talk."

Grant pushed off the desk and threw up his hands in resignation. "Oh, the hell with it."

He shoved his hands in his pockets and crossed to the far side of the room, shaking his head, the tension coiled in his shoulders and limbs almost tangible.

Kelli sensed how much was at stake here and felt a stab of guilt, followed by panic. What if this whole thing backfired? What if Ted didn't like what she had to say?

She'd only intended to help get Grant in the door and have him take over from there. Apparently, Ted had other ideas.

Just do it, she told herself. Follow your instincts. It'll be all right.

She pulled a chair up to the desk and sat down. Lifting the heavy paper and inner tissue covering the first art board, she studied it with a practiced eye. It was a colorful, felt-tip pen layout for a magazine-size ad. Showgirls in brief costumes and spectacular headdresses were encircled by a collage of caricatures of recognizable stars.

The headline, in a swash of red script, stretched across the top in two lines: *Catch A Show. Cassera's Tahoe!* Small lines indicated where additional copy would go below.

After a moment she moved the board aside and glanced at two similar layouts for *TV Guide* ads, and color comps for a brochure and a menu.

"What do you think?" Lazar asked.

Kelli's palms began to perspire. She couldn't be overly critical. She knew Dawson Advertising had prepared the comps, and they hadn't handled this account for six years for nothing.

The ads were well composed, highly professional. But layout was subjective, and these comps were not her style.

"About concept or composition?" she asked.

"Both."

She leaned forward in her chair and took a deep breath. "Composition first. Let's take this ad. There are some good ideas here, but the layout is too busy."

"Busy?" Lazar asked.

"There's too much going on. The collage of stars takes away from your primary focus—the showgirls. I'd recommend using fewer spot illustrations or dropping them altogether, for a clean, sharp look."

Lazar slapped the desktop with his palm. "Exactly what I said!"

"And I'd use a different typeface for the headline. Kabel Ultra or maybe Avant Garde Extra Bold. This script is too hard to read."

Across the room, Kelli saw Grant's hands come out of his pockets. His lips parted in consternation. She flashed him a proud, sprightly grin.

Who are you? he'd probably ask in wonder when this was all over. *How on earth did you pull that off?*

"Do you have any scratch paper?" Kelli asked. "I'll show you what I mean."

"Sure." Ted found a blank notepad in his drawer and handed it to Kelli with a pencil.

Propping the notepad on her knee, she sketched out a new ad, a quick illustration with a bold headline and just enough detail to convey what she was imagining.

"That's much better," Ted agreed when she was finished. "How did you do that so fast?"

Kelli smiled modestly. "If you think I draw fast, you should see the rest of the staff. Believe me, meeting a client's deadline is never a problem."

A little white lie couldn't hurt. With any luck, it might be true.

What was Grant thinking? Why didn't he say anything? She wanted to turn and see his face but didn't dare.

Instead, she answered Ted's questions about possible ideas for a new logo, commented on the color scheme of the brochure, and made a few suggestions for reworking the menu layout. Ted listened with rapt attention, pursing his lips and nodding in agreement.

Grant crossed the room and picked up the sketch she'd drawn. His eyes widened as he studied it. Darting an amazed glance in her direction, he set it aside and went through the art boards one by one.

"Good ideas, Kelli," Ted said when she'd finished her critique.

"Yes." Grant leaned casually back against the desk, watching her. "Very good ideas."

His thigh, lean and hard beneath his gray wool slacks, was just three inches from where her forearm rested on the desk edge. She could almost feel the dynamic energy his body radiated, and the heat of his gaze was like a magnet, drawing her eyes up to his.

But when she looked up, instead of the admiration or appreciation or even grudging acceptance she'd expected to match his words, she met only calm, intense scrutiny with a hint of still-vital anger.

Why? she wondered, alarmed. Couldn't he see that she'd meant only to help him?

"Now tell me," Ted said, "what you think of the overall concept for the ads. Based on what you know about the casino industry, do you think this would be an effective campaign?"

Kelli's mouth went dry. Bob had said they wanted a new look and a new media campaign, but he hadn't given her any details.

She didn't know a thing about the casino business.

Grant glanced at her, then tossed the boards onto the desk and faced Ted. "I think it's a mistake," he said bluntly. "Why place so much emphasis on your shows? I realize entertainment is a big selling factor, but it's such a small part of what you have to offer here in Tahoe."

Grant went on to suggest that the new campaign emphasize the natural environment at Lake Tahoe or try an approach that played up the fun-and-games aspect of gambling.

Ted leaned back in his chair, slanting his eyes at Grant, then chuckled. "Have you been talking to one of our VPs out there, Pembroke?"

"No," Grant said in surprise. "Why?"

Ted stood up. "Never mind. I like your style, Grant. And I like your associate. She's as talented as she is pretty, and with a drawing arm that fast and accurate, I'd say you've found yourself a gold mine." He ripped a clean sheet off the notepad and scribbled a point-by-point listing, then handed it to Grant. "I'd like to see what you can cook up together. This is what we're looking for."

He checked his calendar. "I'm going to be out of town tomorrow, but let's meet back here on Sunday for a tour and final details. Can you get a presentation to me, complete with pricing, in two weeks?"

"Two weeks?" Grant was clearly stunned. He studied Ted's list. "This is a lot to ask for, Ted, with only a two-week turn around."

"I understand. But we're up against a time limit here. Dawson Advertising is putting together a comprehensive presentation by that date, and you'll have to do the same if you want to compete."

After a brief pause, Grant said, "Okay. We'll do it. I'll give you a quote for the presentation work on Sunday, before we go ahead."

"A quote?" Ted let out a small laugh and shook his head. "Sorry if you misunderstood, but this is purely on spec, Grant. We don't pay unless you get the job."

"We don't work on spec." The two men faced each other across the desk. "You pay Dawson for every stroke of his artists' pens, don't you?"

"Yes, but that's—"

"We don't work for free, Ted. We're not that hungry. If you want to see our presentation, you pay for it."

Ted began to protest, then sighed. "All right, just make sure you stay in the ballpark. And you'd better make this worth my while, Grant."

Only the briefest upward twinge of Grant's lips hinted at his delight in their victory. "I will."

"Great." Ted stood up, circled the table, and shook first Grant's hand, then Kelli's. Grant took Ted aside, pulled out his pocket calendar, and set up a meeting time.

Kelli stood idly by, listening but not included, and felt a sudden, ridiculous sense of loss and betrayal.

She'd acted completely on impulse. She'd wanted to give Grant a chance to bid on the account, and she'd achieved that. He could move on without her now, make some excuse to Ted as to why she wasn't working for him anymore. She hadn't expected him to actually hire her.

Had she?

"Let's get back to the party," Ted said. But when they reached the door leading to the presidential suite, Kelli thought of Bob, who was probably still inside, looking for her. She didn't want to run into him now.

"I'm sorry, but I have to go." She thanked Ted once again for the meeting.

"I have to leave too," Grant said, much to her surprise. He gave Ted a parting handshake, and when Ted had disappeared inside, Grant strode down the empty hall in silence beside her until they reached the elevator.

He pushed the call button, leaned against the wall by the doors, and looked at her. Equal measures of curiosity and controlled anger seemed to vie for dominance in his level blue gaze.

"Okay, lady, let's have it," he said calmly. "What's your game?"

She looked at him blankly. "Game?"

"That was quite a performance you gave in there. A real knockout." He shook his head, frowning. "I may be pleased with the way things turned out, but I'm no fool. I don't appreciate being jerked around, and your methods leave a bad taste in my mouth."

Kelli took a step back, stunned into silence. Whatever reaction she'd anticipated from Grant, it wasn't this.

"You said you were meeting your boss at the party, or was it *possibly* your boss," he went on. "I saw you talking with Bob Dawson. Either you're working *for him*, or you're working for *yourself*. Which is it?"

"I'm not working for anyone."

"Come on." He laughed lightly. "I know how Bob operates. He's about as scrupulous as a four-handed pickpocket. The minute you barged in and introduced yourself to Ted, I smelled a rat. At first, I thought you were going to be charming but demonstrate a shocking lack of expertise. Ted would then question my judgment in hiring you and I could kiss the account goodbye. But then you came out with that speech about layout and logos and typefaces ... you had the man eating out of your hand. I guessed then that I must have the scenario all wrong. You were there to wrap Ted around your little finger, to make yourself so indispensable to the account that I'd have no choice but to hire you."

Hot waves of anger and despair surged through her at this unflattering interpretation of her actions. "You don't understand. I wish I could have explained earlier, but there wasn't time."

"There's time now. I've got all night. I'm sure I'd find your story fascinating."

He glanced up at the elevator indicator, which seemed to be stuck on the fifth floor. He pushed the call button again. "What I want to know is, are you in it for yourself? Or are you the Trojan horse, well prepped by Dawson and sent to infiltrate my ranks?"

"Bob Dawson doesn't know anything about this. He offered me a job, but then I realized you were having problems with Ted and I just wanted to help. I see now that it was a mistake. Believe me, the last thing I'd ever do is work for you!"

The doors to the presidential suite burst open. Party hum and laughter filled the hall. Bob Dawson stalked out, followed by two other chattering couples who headed for the elevator.

Bob caught sight of Kelli and Grant and walked slowly toward them, his lips turning up into an icy grin.

"What do you know?" Bob stopped in front of Kelli and shook his head. "He told me, but I didn't believe it. Kelli, I'm disappointed in you. I thought you'd enjoy working for us, especially on this account. But obviously that's not in the cards."

Kelli had no idea what to say, so she clutched her handbag and took a step back, lowering her eyes. The elevator arrived with a ding and she hurried inside, behind the other two couples.

"My hat's off to you, Pembroke," Bob said. "You stole away my new creative director before day one on the job.

Good show. I hope she sticks around for you longer than she did for me."

Grant glanced over his shoulder at Kelli and the closing elevator doors in alarm. "Count on it, Bob." He lunged for the doors, caught them just in time, and stepped in.

Two women were wedged between them in elevator tightness, yet Kelli felt Grant's eyes boring steadily into her as they were whisked downstairs.

Had he changed his tune? Was he going to apologize? Or would he demand an explanation? She saw no reason to give it to him.

When they'd been deposited in the lobby, she swept past him and headed straight for the coat-check counter.

"Kelli, wait."

She had long legs and was a fast walker, despite her high heels, but he matched her stride easily.

"You were on the level, weren't you?"

"Forget it."

"I'm not going to forget it. If you had a job with Dawson, why'd you abandon ship to help me?"

"It doesn't matter."

"It does matter." His hand closed over her arm and he stopped, gently pulling her to a halt beside a busy roulette table. Voices buzzed around her and she could hear a distant ringing bell, a shout, the accompanying clatter of coins. "We need to talk."

The pressure of his fingers sent hot shivers up her arm, and she realized it was the only time he'd touched her other than their brief handshake earlier that evening.

Come on, Kelli, she reproached herself. The man accuses

you of professional conspiracy and you turn to jelly at his touch? "We don't need to talk," she said firmly.

"Yes, we do. I owe you an apology, and you owe me an explanation. Come on, I'm buying you a drink."

"You are *not* buying me a drink. I have nothing to say to you. And I'm *not* thirsty." Which was untrue. She'd barely tasted the champagne at the party and was dying for something cold and frothy. But she wasn't about to let him bully her into going anywhere.

He released her arm with a frustrated gesture. "The Cassera's account means a great deal to me and to my company. I saw you talking to Dawson at the party and I suspected the worst. I'm sorry. I'm grateful for what you did, even if I did come off like a jerk back there."

She fought back a smile. "You did."

"At least we agree on something." He laughed softly. "Look, can we forget the past ten minutes and start fresh? Can we go somewhere and talk? Please?"

In his eyes she saw the same vulnerability, the same warmhearted plea that had made her agree to help him into the party in the first place. She couldn't doubt his sincerity.

Something inside her—like the whirring roulette wheel beside her—went *zing* and spun and turned over. She gave in to her smile.

"Where did you have in mind?"

"So, when I found out the way Bob takes care of his competition, I knew I could never work for him."

Grant sat next to her at a small corner booth in a lounge off the casino floor, and they'd just ordered drinks.

"I don't blame you. I've known that guy for years. This isn't the first time he's tried to stab me in the back."

"I figured you ought to know. And when I overheard Ted, that was the last straw. I thought if I could somehow convince him the rumors weren't true ... I guess it was pretty reckless of me—"

"It was damn reckless. And totally crazy." Grant grinned. "And I'd probably have done the same thing in your shoes."

"You would?"

"I would."

She laughed. "I'm lucky it didn't backfire. I wasn't really thinking ahead or considering the consequences."

"Sometimes spontaneous actions are the best kind. If you think too hard about doing something you can usually talk yourself out of it."

He seemed about to say more, when the waitress arrived with their drinks. Kelli accepted her piña colada gratefully and took a sip of the refreshing coconutty froth.

"Do you live here in Tahoe?" Grant asked.

"No. Seattle." Her brother Kyle, she explained, was building a vacation house at Glenbrook Bay, a sleepy little cove about eleven miles up the road. She'd agreed to stay there for the next three weeks to supervise the details during the final phase of construction.

"What about you? Your agency's in San Francisco?"

He nodded. He'd been in business for himself for the past five years, he told her. He'd had his eye on the casinos, but most of them had in-house agencies or were tied up with long-term contracts.

"When I heard Cassera's was out to bid, I saw my chance. Ted agreed to meet me at the party, and I dashed up here."

"Hardly a *dash*." Kelli knew that San Francisco was a three-hour drive from Tahoe under the best conditions.

"True. I hit so much traffic, I was afraid I'd miss Ted entirely. And I would have, if not for you."

He lifted his Scotch in a salute and took a sip. Leaning back, he stretched one arm across the top of the seat and smiled at her. She smiled back.

She liked the charged directness of his eyes. They approved of her looks, made her feel feminine, attractive, admired.

His complexion was fair, smooth looking, touchable. His shoulders were broad and his arms, beneath the suit jacket, had a look of strength to them. She remembered the rest of his body was slim, trim, gracefully put together.

"That long, huh?"

With an embarrassed flush, Kelli realized she'd missed something he said. What was she doing, thinking about his body? "I'm sorry?"

"I asked how long you've been in advertising?"

"Oh! Six years."

"Have you always been able to draw that fast?"

Matter-of-factly, she said, "Yes. When I was a kid, I won the Quick Draw Contest at the county fair three years in a row."

"The Quick Draw Contest? That's a new one. I take it that's with a pencil, not a revolver?"

She laughed. "Yes."

"What happened after three years?"

"I stopped competing."

"Decided to give the other kids a chance?" He raised his eyebrows, smiling. "Well, you sure impressed the heck out of Ted back there. Not only fast, but damned good."

"Thank you."

"What happened after the county fair? Did you study art in college?"

She nodded, brushing back a lock of her dark reddish-brown hair. "For the past four years I've been working as the art director for T & M in Seattle."

"Thompson and McGuire? I know them. Top-notch firm. You must have worked on the Great Pacific Bank campaign. The one that won the art direction award?"

"You saw it?" she asked, delighted.

"Who could miss it? Imaginative logo, the way the people's profiles blended into the trees. And the colors were both subtle eye-catching." He paused, apparently catching something in her expression. "Was that your design?"

"Yes."

He whistled. "Hot stuff, lady. I'm impressed." He sat forward, his eyes alive with interest. "What else have you done?"

She mentioned a few national campaigns she'd worked on, including a popular color ad for a cruise line that he'd seen and admired. It had showed a leggy young woman in a bikini, relaxing on deck in the hot sun, her tropical drink and festive sombrero lying beside her lounge chair. The headline had read *Bake Sale.*

"I wished I'd done it," Grant said. "Who came up with that headline?"

"I did."

"A woman of many talents. You do award-winning design and write copy, too?"

"Sometimes. I like coming up with the whole concept, but I didn't often get the opportunity."

He regarded her for a moment. "Why'd you leave T & M?"

"I decided to try it on my own." She'd been freelancing for the past couple of months, she explained, when they announced the Advertising Association awards. "The next day Bob Dawson called and asked me to come down for an interview. I had to be in Tahoe anyway for a few weeks, and San Francisco wasn't too far out of the way, so I decided, why not?"

"Why not, indeed. I'll say one thing for Dawson. He's a shrewd businessman. He finds the most talented people in this industry and he goes after them."

Kelli flushed at his praise. In the ensuing silence he lifted his glass, took a drink.

Her gaze dropped to his hands. She couldn't help noticing what long, well-shaped fingers he had. The backs of his hands and wrists, visible beyond the cuffs of his shirt, were lightly dusted with dark, soft-looking hairs. Incredibly masculine.

To distract her thoughts, she plucked the paper umbrella out of the pineapple wedge adorning her glass and twirled it between her fingers.

"You deserved that award," Grant said. "The design was sensational."

"Oh, it was no big deal, really," Kelli said with attempted nonchalance. "The idea came to me in a flash one night while I was taking a bath."

He choked on his drink. Her cheeks grew hot. Did she actually say that?

"Is that where you get all your ideas?" he asked.

She tried to swallow. "A lot of the good ones."

"I'll have to remember that." Grant's lips twitched with amusement.

"What about you?" she asked, in a desperate effort to change the subject. "What have you done that I'd recognize?"

"I guess my favorite over the past year was the Shop N Go chain-store commercials. I had a lot of fun with those."

"You mean those hilarious TV and radio spots with all the little kids?"

"I don't know if I'd call them hilarious—"

"They were! I loved them."

He shrugged. "No big deal. The idea came to me in a flash one night while I was—"

"Oh, stop." She resisted an impulse to punch him playfully on the arm. "You wrote them, then?"

"Wrote them, produced them. I have a top-notch staff, but I like to play my hand on the big projects. Copywriting is my strong suit. That, and rough creative direction."

He went on to name a few of his clients and recent campaigns his agency had worked on, but Kelli unconsciously tuned out his words, her attention drifting instead to the soft gleam of the overhead lights against his dark brown hair, the long eyelashes that veiled his eyes, the way his mouth moved as he spoke.

His lips were perfectly formed, sensuous. It'd be a wonderful mouth for—

"Are you thinking what I'm thinking?"

Kelli blinked, becoming aware that he was gazing at her with disarming intensity. "What?"

"I think you are. I think you know we'd make one hell of a team." His voice was low and deep and seemed to vibrate through her.

"Kelli, come work for me."

CHAPTER 3

Kelli stared at Grant across the table, trying to rein in her wandering thoughts. *We'd make one hell of a team,* he'd said.

She realized she had a completely different sort of team in mind.

"I just picked up three new accounts that are as big and important as Cassera's," Grant went on. "My staff is up to their ears. On my way up here tonight, I realized if I *did* get the chance to bid on this thing, I was going to have to hire some new help. When Ted named his deadline, I knew I was in trouble.

"I've only got two weeks to put this proposal together. I don't usually make a job offer without seeing an artist's portfolio, but I've seen your work. I can use another creative director. Ted already thinks you're working for me, so why not keep it that way?"

After all that had happened that evening, Kelli certainly hadn't expected a job offer from Grant Pembroke. But he was a fascinating man: charming, talented, obviously intelligent. He was respected in the business. She couldn't deny her attraction to him.

And it might be exciting to live and work in San Francisco ....

No, she thought, with sudden determination. She'd already decided *not* to take a job with another agency. She wanted to prove to herself that she could be a success on her own.

If Bob and Grant were both so anxious to hire her, she must have more potential than she realized. She ought to stick to her guns.

"I'm flattered by the offer," she said slowly. "But to tell you the truth, I'm committed to my own freelance business in Seattle."

"Then why did you accept a job with Dawson?"

"I didn't accept the job. I told you, I was just considering it."

"Considering it strongly enough to show up here tonight."

"Yes," she admitted, "but only because my financial situation's been tight. I've thought more about it this evening. I hope, since I won the art direction award, that my business will pick up when I get back home."

"I'm sure it will." He frowned. "Okay. How about freelancing for me, then? Join my staff just until this job's done. I need the help, and your input would be valuable on this proposal. You can drive down to the city tomorrow, look my place over. If you like what you see, you can start on Monday."

Kelli hesitated. It was a tempting proposition. She'd love to work freelance on this job for the casino. She could use the money, and it would look terrific in her portfolio.

But there was her promise to her brother to consider. Reluctantly, she said, "I wish I could. But I can't."

"Why not?"

"I'm committed to staying here at Tahoe for at least another three weeks, until my brother's vacation house is finished."

He stared at her. "Three weeks?"

She nodded, trying not to let her disappointment get the best of her. "Kyle's had a lot of problems since they started construction, because he couldn't be here very often to keep an eye on things. Walls and doorways and windows in the wrong places, they built the stairs and fire-places wrong—you name it.

"The contractor wasn't doing his job and didn't keep to the schedule—the house was supposed to be finished two months ago—and now he took off on vacation, leaving nobody in charge. Kyle is furious. He wants to bring his family up for Christmas, and I agreed to oversee the last phase of the work, to see that it gets done in time."

"Wow. How'd he rope you into coming all the way down from Seattle to do that?"

"He didn't rope me into it. He asked. He lives in Newport Beach and is a very successful businessman. He and his wife didn't have time to come out here right now. I did. I was glad to help." She shrugged, adding lightly, "Then, of course, there was the bribe."

"Bribe?"

"Free and unlimited use of the house, in perpetuity, anytime I want."

"Ah! I'm beginning to understand your motivation." He smiled. "Still, he might be able to find someone else to fill in as contractor. If he knew you had a—"

"There's no time to find someone else. And he's not going to trust this to a stranger. I made a promise, Grant. I wish there was some other way." She sighed. "But there isn't."

Grant fell silent. After a moment he leaned back with a shrug. "Well, I guess that's that. It was worth a shot." He checked his watch. "I'd better hit the road. I have to get back to the city tonight. Let me walk you to your car."

She slid out of the booth and accompanied him across the casino floor to retrieve their coats, feeling let down and mildly dejected. It occurred to her with sudden clarity that if she didn't work for Grant on this job, she might never see him again.

That eventuality didn't seem to bother him, however. In fact, as they crossed the immense back parking lot, she felt certain she saw a speculative gleam in his eyes. She remembered that same look from the moment they met, in front of the elevators. What was he thinking?

She had to hurry to keep up with him. Her cheeks stung from the crisp night air by the time they reached her vehicle.

"That's your car?" Grant's eyes widened with apparent amusement when he caught sight of the old, boxy-looking sedan with its fading paint job in British racing green.

"It is." Kelli proudly unlocked her car door. They didn't sell or service Rovers anymore in the U.S. and most people thought it odd that she owned one.

"This is uncanny." He leaned down to look inside. "I've never—"

"I searched long and hard to find this car," Kelli interjected. "It's the best model Rover ever made, and this one's in tip-top condition." For some reason she felt compelled to defend it. "I just had the seats recovered. Better than new." She would have covered them in real leather, if she could have afforded it, but the soft beige vinyl was a good imitation.

He met her gaze, seeming to choose his words carefully. "It's very nice. Really."

She tossed her purse onto the front seat and waited, realizing she didn't want to talk about her car, but didn't want to say goodbye, either.

He stood nearby in silence, watching her, his lips pressed together in a regretful frown. He lifted his hand as if to touch her cheek, then seemed to think better of it and extended it to her to shake.

"Kelli, you're a terrific lady. Thanks again for your help tonight—for winning Ted over. It was an experience I won't forget."

The knot of disappointment she'd felt as they crossed the parking lot intensified, surging hot and sharp through her chest. Was he really going to just say goodbye? Just like that?

Had she only imagined the glimmer in his eyes each time their gazes had touched? Wasn't he even going to ask for her contact info?

No, she reprimanded herself sternly. She shouldn't be thinking of him that way. After her breakup with Wayne, she'd promised herself to stay free and independent for a while, to avoid any relationships with a man until she'd proven she could make a success of her life on her own.

And she hadn't proven it yet. Far from it.

She shook his hand. "Goodbye."

Before letting her hand go, he gave it a firm squeeze. "Good night, Kelli," he said softly. "I hope we'll meet again sometime."

He smiled and then walked away.

KELLI OPENED her eyes to bright sunlight. She rolled over inside her sleeping bag and picked up her watch from the plywood floor beside her, peering at it through sleep-blurred eyes.

Ten-twenty-eight. Damn! Saturday, the first day no workmen were due to arrive, and she'd overslept.

No point in going skiing now. By the time she got there, half the day would be gone, and the slopes would be crowded with weekend skiers.

It was no wonder she'd slept so late. The night had passed miserably. It wasn't only the eerie, creaking sounds of the empty house that had kept sleep at bay, but thoughts of Grant. His smile, the look in his eyes, and the feel of his hand pressing firmly against hers both times he'd said goodbye.

She wished, now, she hadn't been so definite in her refusal to work with him on the casino campaign.

Couldn't they have come up with some kind of compromise? What if he'd met her here for a few brainstorming sessions? Another artist, back at his agency, could have drawn up the presentation.

No, she realized, that would never work. Another artist couldn't accurately interpret her ideas. She'd seen enough of that in her last job. The finished product never came out the way she'd envisioned.

She sighed. It obviously wasn't meant to be.

Kelli crawled out of the sleeping bag, shivering when her bare feet touched the cold floor. She quickly pulled on a pair of jeans, a woolly pullover, and heavy socks, then stepped into her comfortable suede after-ski boots.

She looked about the large, freshly paneled master bedroom, empty except for her suitcase, sleeping bag, pillows, blankets, air mattress, and the toolbox she'd brought in from the car to attach wall plates over the electrical outlets.

She'd made sure the rooms upstairs were nearly finished before she moved in, so she'd at least have *some* space to herself that was free of sawdust and away from the workmen.

The master bedroom was enormous and especially nice with a rock fireplace, a sliding glass door that led to a second-floor balcony, and a bay window and window seat with a view of the sparkling lake below.

Kelli freshened up at the double sink in the master bathroom, grimacing at the layer of dirt and dust covering the counter, mirror, and tile floor. All the fixtures, including the shower and soaking bathtub with its expanse of surrounding tile, were newly installed and just as dirty.

She'd clean today, she decided. A nice hot bath would be great to sink into tonight, when shadows crept around the house and not even the central heating could keep away the lonely chill.

She'd scrub the tub, the whole bathroom, to a brilliant sheen. She'd done the kitchen the afternoon before, using up all the cleaning supplies and every single rag she'd had the foresight to bring from home.

But after a quick trip to the Laundromat in town and a stop at the supermarket, she'd be set for another day's work.

After a hasty breakfast, she gathered up the bundle of laundry, hopped into her car, and headed south to the town of Stateline, so named because it crossed the Nevada-California border.

The sky was overcast with the promise of snow. Dense pines stretched up the mountainside on her left as she drove. On the opposite side of the winding highway she caught glimpses of the lake through the trees.

Soon she rounded a bend and the row of modern hotels and casinos came into view. People in colorful ski hats and jackets strolled down the sidewalk on both sides, wandering from one casino to another.

She passed the state line into California. The casinos immediately stopped, as if divided by a giant hand, and the business district began. The casual, small-town atmosphere set against the wintry countryside reminded her of Seattle, and she felt right at home.

By one o'clock she'd finished her errands and was loading her groceries into the trunk. A light snow silently drifted from the sky, melting as it hit the pavement. She felt refreshed and invigorated as she breathed in the crisp air.

Kelli climbed into her car and turned the key in the ignition. It sputtered a bit, then died. Cold, she thought. She tried again. This time it started with its usual ease, although the engine idled erratically.

Frowning, she pulled across the supermarket parking lot and turned onto the highway. The engine speed began to waver dangerously from high to low and back again.

Oh no, she thought. She'd only heard that sound once before, when—

The engine died.

She cursed and steered awkwardly to the curb. With experience born of years of practice, she surveyed the situation under the hood, flipped a valve, got back in the car and tried to start it again.

Nothing.

Kelli heaved a frustrated sigh. If only she had her tools and somebody to help her, she could probably get it started. Stupid, she thought. You know better than to go anywhere without your tools.

"Need a hand, lady?"

The familiar, deep voice made her start in surprise.

Grant was looking in at her with concern through the open door. Kelli's heart leaped in delight. Unable to stop her grin, she climbed out and stood beside him in the busy street.

"What are you doing here? I thought you went back to San Francisco last night."

"I did. I came back. I was going to take pictures of the casino, and then …." He paused. "I saw your car, and knew it had to be you."

He looked more handsome than she thought permissible. His jeans, as old, worn, and form-fitting as her own, emphasized the masculine strength of his long, lean legs. His black ski jacket was unzipped, revealing a matching cashmere sweater. Snow touched lightly on his dark brown hair, and his cheeks were rosy from the chill air.

Looking at him, her heart beat as erratically as the recent idling of her car.

"What happened?" He nodded toward the open hood.

"It's the automatic enrichment device. You can't predict when it will give out. If only it had warmed up, I could have turned on the bypass. As it is … you wouldn't happen to have a toolbox handy, would you?"

Five minutes later, Grant was sitting behind her wheel, waiting to turn the ignition, while Kelli was buried elbow deep in the engine of her car.

It seemed he always carried a toolbox in the trunk of his Mercedes. He'd offered to do the dirty work, but she'd insisted he didn't understand her car the way she did.

"Okay," she cried, leaning over the engine and lifting the air filter with grease-stained fingers. "Start her up."

The engine roared to life. She reassembled the air cleaner and wiped her hands on a rag.

"I'll be all right now. Thanks." She brushed snow from her sweater and hair. "Once the engine's warmed up for a while, it'll get me home."

"You don't know that. It might go out on you again."

"I doubt it. I'll need to get a new part eventually, but it'll be fine for a while."

"I don't trust it. I'm going to follow you home."

"You don't have to do that."

"I want to." He paused, then added, "I admit, I have an

ulterior motive. I'd love to see the house your brother is building."

She shrugged in resignation, laughing. How could she say no? He *had* rescued her from the roadside, after all. "Okay. Sure. Let's go."

She climbed behind her wheel and took off. The Mercedes followed close behind as she sped down the highway toward Glenbrook. A few miles out of Cave Rock, the sprinkling of snow stopped, and sun shone through parting clouds.

Kelli turned left on a narrow side road, winding down and around the wooded hillside until she spotted the white flag marker tied to a tree trunk, where she made a sharp right.

The driveway, recently paved, was more like a narrow road. It sloped down through a dense grove of pines and leveled out at the last moment in front of the garage.

They got out of their cars at the same time. "This is some house." Grant was clearly impressed.

"It *is*, isn't it?"

The new redwood siding gleamed beneath the afternoon sun. Rows of huge windows stretched across both floors, reaching clear up to the majestic, peaked roof. Redwood railings edged a second-floor decking that spanned the width of the house and continued around on one side.

The scent of pine hung heavy in the air, and birds twittered in the clusters of tall trees around them. Just twenty yards away, she could hear the soft ebb and flow of the lake lapping against the shore.

"It's still a work in progress, and not exactly a haven of

comfort." She opened her trunk and took out one of the grocery bags. "There isn't a stick of furniture. I'm afraid I can't offer you anything to drink. But you're welcome to come in anyway."

"Thanks." With a wide smile, he took off his ski jacket, slammed his car door, and retrieved the other bag and her bundle of laundry.

She unlocked the carved oak front door and they issued inside. The house smelled of dust and newly cut wood, but she had turned up the thermostat and it was warm and pleasant after the chilly air outside.

When they'd both set down their grocery bags in the kitchen, Kelli led him into the living room.

"Welcome," she said with a grand sweep of her arm, "to my brother's humble vacation retreat."

He whistled, and she laughed in delight. She loved almost everything about the new house, even in its unfinished state, but felt a renewed sense of awe each time she entered this huge, open room.

Filtered sunlight shone in through two dirt-streaked sliding glass doors and through windows high in the vaulted ceiling, illuminating the freshly paneled knotty pine walls and the bare, plywood floor.

A table saw stood against one wall. Long strips of wood molding and assorted boxes of hardware lay in scattered piles. Grant stepped around them, his footsteps echoing in the silent, empty room.

"Incredible," he said. A pair of stained-glass windows were inset on either side of a massive granite fireplace. He stopped to study the intricate depictions of birds surrounded by flowers in colorful shades of glass. "These are exquisite."

"Songbirds. My sister-in-law is a radio disc jockey and that's her favorite symbol. Kyle had them custom-made to surprise her. He's always doing things like that."

Grant looked at her. "He must love his wife very much."

Something in his gaze made her stomach flutter. Her next words stuck in her throat. "He ... does."

Grant offered to help her put the groceries away, and they worked together in the spacious kitchen with its shiny, new appliances.

"Sorry, no cabinet doors." Kelli stashed food in the refrigerator as she gestured toward the oak cabinets lining the walls. "They don't arrive until next week."

"Ah! But you lied." Grant picked up a jar of instant coffee from the countertop. "You said you didn't have anything to drink."

She cringed. "It's horrible, I know, but I bought that as a last resort. There's no coffee maker yet. The small appliances are being sent up just before Christmas."

"I see that you're roughing it here. I can adapt."

"Are you serious? Are you saying that you'd like a cup?"

"Any hot beverage would be welcome right now. But only if *you* have one, too."

Although Kelli felt ridiculous serving instant coffee to a guest, she put on a pot to boil and glanced back at him. She liked his smile. It came so easily.

When he'd spoken of her brother's love for his wife, Grant had sounded sincerely moved, almost wistful. Was he a romantic at heart, as she was? How different that would be from most of the men she'd known.

How different, especially, from Wayne.

If she wasn't careful, she realized, she could easily fall for someone like Grant.

No entangling relationships, she reminded herself. Even her sisters had told her she needed to take a break, to be on her own for a while.

"So, you're the acting contractor now? You must have experience in house construction?"

"No. But I took a few classes in architectural drafting in college. I can read a blueprint, and Kyle left a detailed list of instructions. I'm just supposed to make sure the subcontractors come out on schedule and do what they're supposed to do, and that everything is delivered and installed as ordered."

"Your brother is lucky to have you on the job."

"I guess, but I don't mind helping out. He's a great guy." She stacked soup cans in an open cupboard. "Ever since he became a father last year, he's been cutting down on his business trips and spending more time at home. My sister-in-law can't spare much time away from the radio station. A week over the holidays—that's all the time they've got this year, and this is sort of my Christmas present to them. Besides, I have a special interest in this house."

"A special interest?" He leaned on the counter barely an inch away from her. "You mean besides free and unlimited use of the house, in perpetuity?"

His nearness distracted her and set her heart racing. "Yes."

"What kind of special interest?"

"I helped with the initial design."

"You design houses, too?"

"No." He was standing so close she became aware of the mild, woodsy scent of his aftershave. "But when Kyle told me he wanted a house on the lake, I envisioned the place in my mind. I had to put it on paper. So, I did a few interior and exterior watercolors for him, and then I sketched out a rough floor plan. He liked it so much he told the architect to build it, more or less, the way I'd drawn it."

"You never cease to amaze me, Kelli," he said softly. "This house is beautiful."

Grant's blue eyes caught hers and held, with a gleam so intense it seemed he had touched her. Taking a deep breath to steady herself, she stepped back and smiled brightly. "Would you like to see the rest of it?"

KELLI MADE the coffee in disposable cups which they took with them. After showing him the nearly finished rooms on the lower floor, they headed upstairs. When they reached the master suite where she was camping out, he said, "Hey, you really *are* living here."

"Kyle offered to put me up at a hotel, but I told him there was no point in spending the money. Especially since he wanted me to be here all day to admit and oversee the workmen, who have a nasty habit of starting at dawn. They're finished in this room, at least, except for paint and carpet."

"It can't be very comfortable, without any furniture. Are you really sleeping on the floor?"

She shrugged. "I'm fine with the floor. I was a Girl Scout. Growing up, nearly every summer I spent a month at camp, sleeping in a tent or outdoors, sometimes on ground as hard as a rock. In comparison—with this fancy, double air mattress my brother ordered for me—this is the Ritz."

"Where do you eat?"

"At the kitchen counter. Or on the—"

"—floor," he finished with her. They shared a grin.

"Or at one of the casinos," she added. "Weekday breakfast special: bacon, eggs, and pancakes, a dollar ninety-nine. You can't beat it."

"Unless you drop five bucks in the slot machines on your way out. Which is their hope and intention."

"Five bucks? Never. My limit is two."

"Big spender."

"Sometimes I risk more. If the mood grabs me."

His gaze met hers. "I noticed," he said softly.

She supposed he was thinking about the way she'd agreed to help him into the party the night before, and the way she'd barged in on his conversation with Ted Lazar. But his expression seemed to indicate he was thinking of something else, too. Something in the future, something far more intimate.

Her insides fluttered wildly, and she moved to the bay window. Outside, beyond a narrow strip of white beach, sunlight danced on the rippling water. Puffy white clouds gathered low in the clear blue sky over distant, snow-capped Mount Tallac.

"I haven't always been so impulsive." She strained to keep her voice light.

"No? What were you like before?" he asked from behind.

"Kind of … shy and retiring."

"That's hard to believe." His hands closed over her shoulders. The unexpected touch sent a spark of electricity racing through her. "You seem anything but shy and retiring."

She turned around to face him and gazed up into his captivating eyes, which didn't attempt to disguise his attraction to her. Her pulse pounded. He didn't intend to kiss her … did he?

Did she want him to?

"I promised myself, once," he said, his voice husky, "that I'd never mix business with pleasure. I can see, in your case, that's not going to be easy to do."

She glanced away, confused, willing her heart to resume its natural cadence. Why was he talking about business, when she was thinking about pleasure?

He released her and took a step back. "Kelli, I've been doing some thinking. I have a proposition for you."

"A proposition?"

"If you can't come to San Francisco and work freelance for me, how about if I come up here and work with you?"

It was the last thing she'd expected him to say. "What do you mean? You want to hold a brainstorming session, like I suggested last night?"

"More than that. I'm talking about putting together the whole creative part of the presentation here. Just you and me."

"Just you and me?" she repeated, astonished.

"If I'm going to bid on the Cassera's job, I need someone like you. You can't leave Tahoe. Which only leaves me this option. I think it could work. A good chunk of this proposal is the quote. I can turn that over to my staff, while we concentrate on the creative end.

"Ted wants the campaign to focus on two things: gambling and the environment. Working up here would have a lot of advantages. The casino's here for research and sudden inspiration if we need it. And all this natural beauty's bound to generate some great creativity."

Kelli hardly knew to say. "Where would we work?"

"I was going to suggest that we work at Cassera's. I'll get a suite at the hotel. You could oversee everything with the construction crew every morning before you come out. But—"

She shook her head. "I should be here as much as I can. The details in these last weeks are too important. Deliveries are made and questions can come up at any hour. If the workers put in the wrong sink or paint a room the wrong color, it can cause extensive delays and get really expensive."

"I figured you'd say that. So, let's go to Plan B. Let's work here."

Now she was truly flabbergasted. "You want to work *here*? In this unfinished house?"

"Why not?" He nodded toward the bay window. "This room's perfect to work in. Great natural light."

"Grant. This is crazy."

"It's not crazy. It's thinking outside the box. I told you last night: my creative people are overloaded, and I don't want to pull them off the jobs they're working on. I expected Ted to give me more time on this. I was hoping for a month. When he named his deadline … honestly, I didn't know how on earth I'd be able to pull it off.

"But I saw the kind of work you can do. If we put our heads together, we ought to be able to come up with a package that sizzles in a couple of weeks. I'll pay you top Bay Area wages as a free-lance consultant." He named a fee. "Plus, a thousand-dollar bonus if we win the account."

Kelli took a sharp breath. She only charged her clients in Seattle half the rate he'd offered—and work was intermittent. Two weeks at that hourly rate would be a small fortune. She could afford to buy new equipment, maybe even rent a small office when she got back home.

"It's an intriguing proposition," she said slowly. "But can you really be away from your agency for two weeks?"

"It's no different than if I took a vacation. I can keep tabs on everything as long as I'm near a phone." He nodded towards a corner, where the new phone was already plugged in and waiting. "If a problem comes up, I can go back to the city any time. After we work up the rough creative, you can always do the comps on your own."

His plans were tumbling out so fast it made her dizzy. "But I don't have any equipment here. I'd need a drafting table, lights, art supplies …."

"I'll bring up everything we need in the company van tomorrow."

Kelli sat down on the window seat, trying to think. Something wasn't right about this. He made it sound so easy. Too easy.

Glancing at the bare plywood floor, she said, "Wait, Grant. You're forgetting something. We can't work here. A pack of carpenters are coming on Monday. All that sawdust and hammering make a racket like you can't believe."

"You said they're finished upstairs, right?"

"Yes, but the painters come after that. Upstairs *and* down. Then the hardwood floors and carpet go in. Have you ever heard anyone put in a hardwood floor quietly? We couldn't get any work done here if we tried."

"Noise doesn't bother me. If it gets to you, though, we can always take a break. Do some research to spark the creative juices. Are you any good at blackjack?"

"Grant!" She stood up. "You're not listening. There will be interruptions—"

"Par for the course. I'm pulled in at least six different directions on any given day."

"We'll be in the way. Whatever equipment you bring up would have to be moved when they lay the carpet in here."

"When's that?"

"A week from Wednesday." Two days before the proposal was due.

"By then we'll be done."

"How can you be so sure?"

"We only need a couple of days of research. A day or two of brainstorming. Three days to whip up the collateral materials and a few more to come up with the ads. Ten days. Eleven, max."

He crossed to stand in front of her, leaning one hand on the wall as he smiled down at her. "We ought to have at least two days to spare. And just think," he said, raising his eyebrows above teasing eyes, "what we could do with a little free time."

She turned away, cheeks warming at his unspoken

thoughts. What was he implying? Why was he going to so much trouble to work with her?

His proposal was completely unorthodox. There must be plenty of artists in San Francisco who'd jump at the chance to work on this presentation. She sensed he was attracted to her, but that couldn't be the only reason. He clearly had faith in her abilities; he wouldn't risk such a vital account on someone whose work he didn't trust.

Uncertainly, she said, "I'd like to do it, Grant, but I have to check with my brother first. He might not be thrilled about me turning his master bedroom into an advertising studio before he's even had a chance to move in."

"It's all right. He's agreed to the whole thing."

She stared at him. "What? How could he?"

"I called him this morning."

"You *called my brother?*" She was dumbfounded. "How on earth did you—"

"You told me his name and where he lives. Directory assistance did the rest. I didn't want to put you in the position of having to say yes or no for him, so I decided to check with him first."

It took a moment to sink in. "But ... if you already talked to Kyle ... he must have given you the phone number here. You could have called me."

"I didn't want to bring this up on the phone, Kelli. I wanted to see the place first, make sure it was feasible, and then talk in person."

"So, you're saying you were on your way up to the house today, to talk to me, when—"

"—when I saw your car at the side of the road. Yes."

Irritation prickled through her. "You conveniently

forgot to mention that. You said you were here to take pictures of the casino."

"I was."

"You made me think we met by chance, that I led you here of my own free will."

"You did."

"I did not! You insisted on following."

"I said I'd love to see the house, and you agreed," he said quietly.

"That's lying by omission." Kelli glared at him. He must have thought of this last night, before he said goodbye. That explained the little gleam she'd noticed in his eyes.

He'd gotten Kyle's permission without even consulting her. Today, while he was bantering with her in the kitchen, he was actually sizing the place up to see if he wanted to work here with her. And he'd never said a word.

The situation was all too familiar. Memories she'd tried to bury came flooding back. Memories of another man who'd planned every single thing in her life and made all her decisions without ever asking her. "I found us a new apartment today," Wayne had said, and was surprised when she wanted to see it before signing the lease.

Didn't want to get you involved in all that paperwork, honey. It's taken care of. We move in next week.

Kelli headed for the door. "Your plan is a little too neat for me, Grant. I've had about as much of domineering, overbearing men as I can take. Thanks, but no thanks."

"Domineering?" Grant asked, coming after her. "Overbearing? *Moi?*"

"Yes! And don't get condescending on me." She stomped

down the stairs and turned in the entryway to face him, her chest tight with fury.

"My last boyfriend was exactly like you. A Mr. My-Way-or-the-Highway. So was my boss. I finally got out from under their thumbs, and I'm not about to put up with that again. I don't like having my life and my work prearranged for me. I don't like people stepping in and taking over. I like to have some say in what I do. I like to be asked."

"Seems to me," Grant said, his own temper rising, "you don't have any scruples about stepping in and interfering in other people's lives. You didn't lose a minute's sleep over the stunt you pulled on me with Ted Lazar, did you? All for a good cause, right? If you can dish it out, you've got to learn to take it."

Kelli felt a stab of guilt and fell silent.

"You seemed interested in the work last night," he continued fervently. "The only thing stopping you, I thought, was your obligation here. I arranged this with your brother ahead of time to make things easier for you—not to exercise some kind of power trip."

"Then why didn't you tell me about it sooner?"

"I was going to tell you as soon as we got here. But I got ... distracted." His eyes caught and held hers.

She hesitated, reading the unspoken message in his gaze, unable to deny how much his presence distracted *her*.

"If you'll simmer down and think about this," he added, "it's not just for my benefit. It's a good opportunity for you, a showcase for your talent."

It was true. She'd worked hard over the past six months to start her own business, be her own boss, and she was fed up with other people calling the shots. But the job for Cassera's *was* a terrific opportunity. Only a prominent agency could secure a client of that magnitude.

She needed the work and needed the money. How could she turn it down?

She felt Grant's eyes on her, watching her closely, as if sensing her change in mood. She tried to imagine what it would be like to work with him. The presentation for the casino would be an exciting challenge. It would be fun to toss ideas back and forth with Grant.

She could envision the creative energy that might flow between them. He was a writer, a leader, a project coordinator. She was an artist. They might indeed make a good team.

She took a deep, wavering breath. "It's just for two weeks, right?"

"Yep."

"Okay. Two weeks. It's a deal."

"Great." He grinned, his eyes a brilliant blue in the sunlit hallway as he stuck out his hand. "Welcome aboard."

It was the third time they'd shaken hands, she realized —and just as before, the warmth of his firm grip sent a tingle dancing up her arm.

"I'll reserve a room at the hotel and be back here with the equipment some time tomorrow morning. We'll unload, set up, and then head down to the casino for my two o'clock meeting with Ted Lazar."

A few minutes later they said goodbye and Kelli shut the front door, her mind spinning. It had all happened so fast. She needed to call Kyle right away, to confirm his approval. But if everything Grant said was true, it ought to be clear sailing.

It was only after she heard Grant's car drive away that a new problem came to mind. One that, she realized, could easily turn the weeks to come into a disaster.

How could she work side by side with Grant for two solid weeks, locked up alone in this house? A high-voltage charge seemed to flow between them.

At times, she'd barely been able to concentrate on their conversation. How would she be able to concentrate on her work?

CHAPTER 4

The decor at Cassera's Tahoe Hotel and Casino had an Alpine flair that Kelli found fresh and inviting.

Sunday afternoon she toured the facility with Grant and Ted, saw the back offices and inner sanctums that the average guest was never allowed to see, and met staff from all parts of the business. She enjoyed herself immensely.

Ted complained that the hotel lobby was too bland and needed sprucing up, but when he showed them the rotating bar in the center of the casino, which was modeled after a German beer garden, he beamed with pride.

There were three restaurants: gourmet French, an immense buffet that changed the nationality of its cuisine each night of the week, and the Swiss Chalet coffee shop that served everything from bacon and eggs to cheese fondue.

"Our showroom has never been a money-maker," Ted explained when he'd brought them upstairs to his private dining room for an early dinner. "The big-name talent is getting more expensive all the time. We've only kept it this long because it draws crowds to the gaming tables. We'll still have a few small showrooms going, but we've decided to do away with the dinner show starting this spring."

Kelli remembered how, at their first meeting, Grant suggested they'd be better off steering away from so much emphasis on their shows, and she saw now why Ted had been so impressed.

"Dawson's given us enough ads promoting the buffet special to last another six years, so you don't need to cover that angle," Ted explained. "What I want is a couple of different campaigns, one that concentrates on sports and the great outdoors, and one that highlights the fun of gambling. Dawson's been avoiding ads that play up gambling because they're so hard to do."

Kelli nodded, remembering that it was illegal to advertise gambling in California. "Can we show people at the tables? Or rolling the dice?"

"You have to be careful how you do it," Grant answered. "The lower the profile, the better."

"That's right," Ted agreed. "We can't promise anyone they'll win. We can allude to it in a subtle way, just so long as we don't come straight out and talk about it."

Some trick, Kelli thought, replacing her monogrammed coffee cup in its saucer. Here was a challenge she'd never encountered before. How did you advertise something if you couldn't even mention it?

When they returned to Ted's office and reviewed the requirements for the final presentation, Kelli was struck for the first time by the sheer volume of the workload.

They wanted a new logo—something completely

different and original, according to Ted—to emphasize their Alpine theme. Two layouts in color for a stationery package to go with it. Pencil comprehensives with a fresh, new look for their collateral materials, all to work around the new logo.

Rough comps for a media campaign with two themes and five or six different creative approaches. No TV and radio; just newspaper, magazines, billboards. Complete copy for a couple of them, and pricing for all of that.

She bit her lower lip, thinking, *what a tall order*. An exciting order, but a tall one, nevertheless. Grant's staff would do the quote, but the creative was up to the two of them. And everything was due before Ted's board-of-directors meeting a week from Friday, less than two weeks away.

"No problem," Grant said.

Kelli glanced at him, marveling at his self-composure. How could he be so confident they'd finish in time? Grant handed Ted a neatly typed form with his quote for their presentation, and Ted sucked in his breath, shook his head slowly and muttered something, then stood up and stuck out his hand.

"Okay, Grant. Let's do it." When he'd shaken Kelli's hand, he said, "I think we're all set. The only place I haven't really shown you is the casino floor, but I'm out of time today." He picked up his phone. "Let me see if—"

"Relax, Ted," Grant said. "We don't need a tour guide. I've been playing blackjack here since I was seventeen."

Ted chuckled and clapped Grant on the back as he walked them to the door. "You're lucky we never checked your ID."

The moment they stepped out of the elevator Kelli felt the air of nighttime excitement in the crowded casino. Slot machines whirred and jangled, mingling with the murmur of laughter and voices. The blackjack tables were busy, and people clustered around the roulette and craps tables.

"Have you spent much time in a casino?" Grant asked.

Kelli shook her head. "This is my first trip to Tahoe. Friday night was the one and only time I'd ever set foot in a casino, and all I had a chance to play were the slot machines."

"Let's take a look around, then." Grant told her to keep in mind that the campaign proposal had to concentrate on the fun, capture the excitement of the place in words and in pictures. "We've got to lure people here who might be just a little bit nervous about gambling."

Like me, Kelli thought. "Have you really been gambling here since you were seventeen?"

"Yep. My parents brought us up here every summer ever since I can remember, and we'd snow ski three or four times a year, too. I started sneaking in here when I was— oh, about twelve, I guess. I watched and listened and learned. They don't usually bother you when you're underage as long as you don't try to play."

"And now? Do you play a lot?"

"No. It takes too long to earn a dollar. There's no fun in watching it slip through your fingers. But once in a while, if you know what you're doing and limit the amount you're going to spend, you can have a great time."

She stopped beside a silver-dollar slot machine as big as a refrigerator, called Fun Fred. A hard hat topped the huge, animated head that housed the money slot and giant cylinders, and the side lever was fashioned like a construction worker's arm.

"This guy," she said, "needs a new name."

"You don't like Fun Fred?"

She shook her head. "On Friday I dropped five dollars into that twelve-inch grin of his. It wasn't fun. He ate them all."

"Well, there goes my idea for one of the newspapers ads. I was going to show a beautiful woman pulling Fred's handle." He painted an imaginary banner through the air with one hand. "With the headline: For a good time, call Fred."

They laughed together.

"I'll talk to the casino manager," Grant joked, "see if he can rename the guy Hungry Harry."

"Or Benny the Bandit."

"In all the years I've been here, I've only seen one person win on that infernal machine. Five hundred dollars. It was something. The ringing bell, all those coins spilling out. Almost enough to turn me into a slots player."

"Almost? You mean you never play the slots?"

"Never. They have the worst odds of any game in the house."

"Why? Are they preset to pay off only a certain percentage?"

"Exactly. Which is why Ted wants Cassera's known as *the* place to play slots. Anyway, they're too monotonous for me. If I'm going to play, I want a game that requires some concentration, a little skill."

With one hand at her elbow he propelled her forward

to the gaming tables. "Come on. I'll explain how a few of the games work."

For the next half hour, Grant went over the basic concepts of keno, roulette, and baccarat, explaining the denominations for the colored chips. At the craps table, half a dozen players lined the sides, all eyes intent on a gray-haired man in an aloha shirt who shook a pair of dice in cupped hands, murmuring over and over to himself under his breath.

Kelli stopped to watch. The table was long and narrow with high, padded sides. White lines divided a field of green felt into an array of numbered sections.

"Do you want to play?" Grant asked beside her.

Kelli shook her head. "I wouldn't have the faintest idea what I was doing."

"Neither do most of the people around here. I'll explain as you go."

"I'd lose all my money in two seconds."

"I thought you liked the idea of living dangerously," Grant teased.

"I do. Sometimes." She'd promised herself to overcome her cautious nature, to participate in life, not stand on the sidelines while it marched by. But what little money she'd brought had to last for at least two more weeks, until Grant paid her for her part in the project.

"Right now, I'd rather watch."

"Come on six," the man cried, throwing the dice. The small crowd groaned. The dealer—cool and businesslike in a black skirt, white blouse, and black bow tie—gathered the chips from the table with a hooked stick. "Any craps?" she called out. "Any craps?"

A thin, snowy-haired woman slid up onto the stool next to Kelli and pulled a stack of blue chips from her purse.

"Place all bets," said the dealer. "Any craps? Hard ways? Come? Don't come?"

"That's why I play this game." The old woman winked mischievously. "I love it when they talk dirty."

Grant grinned and leaned on the side of the table next to Kelli. "I've got our headline," he said in a low voice. "Cassera's: Crappiest Game in Town."

Kelli joined in his laughter, and when his arm brushed hers, the brief touch sent that familiar, warm glow spreading through her. Aloha Shirt rolled again and apparently won. Kelli cheered along with the rest of the crowd.

"Would you like to roll the dice?" the dealer asked Kelli after the man had gathered his chips and left.

Kelli shook her head. "No, thank you."

Grant reached into his pocket, pulled out three twenty-dollar bills, and tossed them on the table. "Yes, she would."

Alarmed, Kelli said, "I can't gamble with your money."

"Yes, you can."

"I can't," she insisted.

"Then we'll say it's company funds. All part of the job. Think of it as research."

She shook her head, but it was too late. The dealer placed a stack of chips in front of her.

Grant took her hand with gentle firmness and turned it over, placing the dice in her palm. "The odds are better here than almost any other game, as long as you avoid the propositions."

"Propositions? What does that mean?"

"See that area in the center of the craps layout, where

the high payouts are printed? The Horn bet, the One Roll bets, and so on? Those are the proposition bets, and they're some of the worst bets in the game. All of them have a very high house edge. I never play them. Just play the Pass/Don't Pass Line."

In confusion, she watched him put a five-dollar chip in an area marked Pass, and then the dealer was telling her to go ahead and shoot.

"Make sure the dice hit the back wall," Grant said, standing close beside her, "or it's not legal."

Kelli's heart began to pound, as much from Grant's nearness as from her nervous anticipation about the game. She still had no idea what she was doing.

Pretend it's a Frisbee, she thought, shaking the dice and tossing them hard. They bounced against the side and shot back, finally coming to a stop at the center of the table.

"Nice arm," Grant commented.

"Three," said the dealer, instantly clearing most of the chips off the table.

"What happened?" Kelli asked.

Grant's response was low and deep against her ear. "You lost."

"Just like that?"

"Just like that."

She shook her head. "Wow. Now *this* is what I call fun."

He laughed softly. "Don't be a sore loser. Try it again."

"You *like* to lose money?"

"On the Pass Line," Grant said calmly, "you only lose if you roll two, three, or twelve on the first roll. You win on seven or eleven. Put out another bet."

She hesitated, then put a three-dollar bet on the Pass Line.

"Twelve," said the dealer after Kelli rolled. "House wins." She cleared off the table.

"I have an idea." Kelli turned to Grant with a bright smile. "After we're through here, why don't we go back to the house and burn a handful of twenty-dollar bills in the fireplace? Wouldn't that be fun?"

Grant shot her a disparaging look. "Just stick to the Pass Line. It's bound to pay off sooner or later."

"Okay, fine. But this time, I'm only going to bet a dollar. In my family, whenever you make a dollar bet, you win."

Kelli threw a seven. "I won!" she cried with delight. All around her were bright colors, gleaming lights, smiling people, murmuring voices, clatters and clinks and bells. She felt a vibrant rush of excitement, wanted to embrace it all. Why hadn't she had the nerve to try this before?

Grant grinned. "See? I told you it'd pay off if you stuck with it."

Kelli's exhilaration dissipated, however, as she watched the dealer pay off the other players in tall stacks, then match her single-dollar chip on the table. When you bet small, you win small, she realized. No fun in that.

The old woman next to her placed a one-inch stack of five-dollar chips on the Pass Line. "I just won this at blackjack," she said, patting Kelli on the arm, "so don't disappoint me, honey."

"I'll try not to." With sudden conviction Kelli shoved out her remaining chips, fifty-three dollars in all.

Grant's grin faded as she picked up the dice. "You're betting the whole thing?"

"Sure," she said loftily.

"I wouldn't," he cautioned.

"Why not? Who said I ought to live dangerously?"

Grant began to protest again, but she threw the dice.

"Ten," said the dealer. "Your point."

Uncertain what that meant, Kelli turned to Grant. He shook his head, laughing silently. "Okay, hot shot. Keep shooting. You're looking for another ten. If you roll your point before you roll a seven, you win even money."

"And if I roll a seven first?"

"You lose."

Perspiration beaded Kelli's neck and brow. A glance the length of the table showed several bets riding. If she rolled a seven, she wouldn't be the only one losing money.

Concentrate, she told herself. *Clear your mind. Visualize only a ten.* She threw the dice, again and again.

"Come on, ten!" someone called out.

"Give me that ten!"

She leaned forward and flung the dice one more time with a dramatic sweep of her arm.

The crowd groaned. A three and a four. She'd lost. She watched the dealer clear the table, feeling hollow inside with disappointment and embarrassment. Fifty-three dollars! Why had she bet so much?

Kelli managed a brief smile and thanked the dealer before moving away from the table.

"Hey, don't worry about it," Grant said, seeing her forlorn expression. "It's all part of the game. Let's try something where we really have a chance."

"Such as?" she asked skeptically.

"Blackjack." He stopped at a nearby table and gestured toward an open stool.

She frowned dejectedly. She knew how to play black-jack, used to beat her brother and sisters all the time for sticks of gum. But this time it was for real.

"I've lost enough for today. If we're going to be holed up in that house for two weeks, I've got grocery shopping to do, and the stores are about to close."

He shrugged. "Okay. But we're coming back before the week is out. I'm going to make sure you win back every penny you lost."

"Why did you tell me not to bet so much?" she asked as they drove back in Grant's van. "How did you know I'd lose?"

"I didn't. But craps is all luck. Betting a few dollars is one thing, but you were so hesitant in the beginning, I didn't want you to feel guilty if you lost."

She sighed. "I guess I just got caught up in the excite-ment of it. It was so much fun when I won."

"That's the whole point. That's why I wanted you to play. Remember the excitement, how it felt to win. Because somehow—without making any promises—we've got to bottle and sell that to the public."

Next morning, Kelli awoke to the sound of a car pulling into the driveway.

She rubbed her eyes, at first not certain where she was. A pile of cardboard boxes came into view.

She sat up with a start, remembering that she'd moved

her makeshift bed to a far corner of the master bedroom the day before, when they'd unloaded Grant's van. In the light of early morning, she surveyed with renewed amazement the temporary studio that took up nearly half the room.

Two drafting tables with attached, adjustable-arm lamps now faced the bay window. Between them, a taboret —a storage unit the size of a two-drawer file cabinet—held a lazy Susan filled with graphics tools. Everything from Exacto knives and burnishers to a complete set of Rapidograph pens.

A portable opaque projector for enlarging and reducing images sat atop a folding table, next to a waxer, a box of assorted felt-tip pens, and a stack of typographer's books. Scattered packing boxes held crescent board, pads of tracing paper, and other supplies.

He'd even brought an electric typewriter, typing table, and two swivel chairs.

She could see why Grant had earned a reputation for being thorough. She hadn't expected a setup anywhere near so elaborate on such short notice.

A knock sounded at the door. A glance at her watch told her it was only six-thirty. Damn those workmen, anyway. Why did they have to start so early?

She scrambled out of her sleeping bag, gooseflesh covering her skin as she pulled jeans and a white turtleneck sweater over her skintight long johns. She fingercombed her hair and, in her stocking feet, hurried down the stairs, careful to sidestep the piles of discarded nails, pieces of drywall, and other debris scattered about.

It was just as cold downstairs as up, and she stopped to adjust the thermostat before throwing open the door.

"Hi," Grant said.

Kelli blinked in surprise. Silhouetted by the soft early light, Grant's shoulders seemed even broader, his waist beneath his black sweater even trimmer, his legs incredibly lean and strong. His cheeks glowed as if morning air were a tonic.

His features reminded her of a statue she'd once seen of a Roman warrior. He had the same masculine cut to his jaw, the same perfectly straight nose, the same beautifully formed lips, as if chiseled out of stone by a master.

The night before, after they'd returned from the casino, he'd taken her hand in his and had given it a warm squeeze as they stood at the door.

"Good night, Kelli Ann," he'd said quietly, before turning to walk down the drive. From the darkness, his voice had come back to her again, soft and deep, like a caress. "Pleasant dreams."

She'd watched the gleam of his taillights disappear and had stood with the door open to the cold night air for quite some time before it had occurred to her to close it. The tingling she'd felt from the gentle pressure of his hand on hers had lingered in her mind throughout the night.

How easy, she thought, staring at him now, it would be to fall for this man.

Be honest, Kelli. You're already halfway there.

She scolded herself to stop thinking of him that way. She didn't want to get involved with anyone right now, and even if she did, it couldn't be with Grant.

They had made a deal to work together. A two-week

deal. Their relationship had to be professional, nothing more.

"You were expecting someone else, maybe?" He sounded breezy and self-assured. The opposite of the way she felt.

She laughed self-consciously and let him in, closed the door. "I expected to see three men wearing dirty jeans and carrying toolboxes. I didn't think you'd be here so early."

"I told you I'd be back with breakfast in the morning."

For the first time, she noticed he was carrying a paper bag and a small tray with two ceramic mugs covered with foil. "This isn't morning. This is predawn. My stomach doesn't wake up for another three hours yet."

"Oh. Sorry. I'm an early riser by habit. If you want to go back to sleep, I can come back in a couple of hours."

"That's okay." The tantalizing aroma of strong coffee filled the room. "I can forgive you when you bring coffee that smells like this."

Unable to resist, she took one of the mugs from his tray, uncovered it, and breathed in deeply, letting the steamy rich scent fill her senses. "Mmm. Take-out coffee never smelled so good. Where did you find it?"

"At a great little coffee shop near the hotel. Best coffee in the town, freshly brewed. They don't do take-out, unfortunately. I had to promise on bended knee to return the tray and mugs."

"Please tell them how much I appreciate the loan. And thank you for going to the trouble."

"You're welcome. I aim to please."

"How's the hotel?"

"Nice. The bed's not as comfortable as I'd like, but I'll live."

"At least you *have* a bed, which is more than I've got."

His eyes twinkled devilishly, and he leaned closer. "Should I make the obvious rejoinder?"

She realized at once what that would be: *You're welcome to join me in mine.* Her cheeks grew warm. "Let's not go there." She quickly turned toward the staircase, bringing her coffee with her. "I'd better go get freshened up. You're welcome to come upstairs in the meantime."

A few minutes later she found Grant sitting astride a stool at one of the drafting tables, paging through a book of color photographs of the Lake Tahoe area. He motioned toward the paper bag on the table. "Help yourself."

Inside she found two egg and cheese sandwiches on toasted bagels. *Food, the best kind of distraction. Yay!* "This looks great. Thanks." She wasted no time taking a bite.

"I thought you weren't hungry this early," he commented, still bent over his book and clearly amused.

"My appetite suddenly returned." Chewing, she crossed to stand behind him. He'd taped a brochure and letterhead to the table and had circled the existing Cassera's logo. "Where do you want to start? With the new logo?"

"Yes. Let's work up two or three ideas and see how they look with the collateral materials. If we can figure out the size and colors for all the pieces today, I can call my office tomorrow and have them start working up printing prices."

They ate the sandwiches and sipped coffee as they discussed possible directions for the new logo. Just as Kelli was about to sit down and sketch out an idea, the doorbell rang.

"Morning," said the man at the front door when she ran down to answer it. He had a ruddy face and wore a baggy jumpsuit beneath his heavy jacket. "I'm John McClellan. You Mrs. Harrison?"

"Miss Harrison. I'm taking care of things for my brother."

"Sorry to bother you so early. I'm the painter." He squinted at his clipboard. "I've got an order here to start the day after tomorrow. I have to figure out how much paint I need."

"No problem." Kelli hurried him inside. "Take a look around. If you need me, I'll be upstairs."

He tramped down the hall, scribbling notes. She was about to head upstairs when the doorbell rang again.

It was the carpenters. They entered and shrugged out of their jackets.

"You're here bright and early." Kelli was grateful Grant had arrived as early as he did to wake her up.

"Thought we'd better get moving." Larry, the oldest and tallest of the three men, was clad in a stained work shirt and faded jeans. "Weather report says snow the end of the week. We want to be done and out of here long before that."

Kelli frowned as she hurried back up the stairs. If it snowed, she'd have to get the driveway plowed, or workmen wouldn't be able to reach the house.

In the master bedroom—which she now thought of as the "studio"—Grant still stood at the drafting table, tapping a pencil against the open page of a book of typefaces. At his feet were a few crumpled wads of paper.

"You're back just in time," he remarked. "How about this typeface for the logo? With a graphic of a snowflake or pines? I made a few attempts. Nothing's worked so far."

Kelli sat down and glanced through the book on Tahoe, seeking inspiration. After a while, she said: "Oh! I have an idea."

She grabbed a fresh sheet of tracing paper. Working fast, she sketched a pine tree, then blended it with the "C" in *Cassera's*. When she was finished, she sat back, unsatisfied.

Grant leaned one elbow on his table, chin on his hand, watching her with open admiration.

"It's not really any good," she said honestly.

"No. But it's not that bad, either. What's amazing is how fast you drew it."

"I can't take credit for my speed. It's not something I've worked hard to develop. It's just ... there."

"Take credit for it anyway, Kelli Ann. It's an extraordinary talent. And I'm beginning to think it'll come in very handy on this proposal."

"*If* we hit on the right ideas."

"We will." Grant picked up his pencil. "Why don't you try this?" He leaned over her drawing and began to sketch.

Kelli had to stifle a sharp breath. His frame lightly brushed up against her back as he worked. Her entire body seemed sensitized by the contact, and her pulse raced.

Very inconvenient, she thought—this dramatic, sexually charged response to his simplest touch.

"Excuse me." The painter poked his head in the open

doorway, startling Kelli so much she jumped sideways off her stool. "It says here Mr. Harrison wants white everywhere there's no paneling. I'm to leave the choice of paint color up to you. Can you take a look at these paint charts?"

"Sure," Kelli replied, both sorry and relieved at the interruption.

The painter paused and held up a hand. "Hold on, I've got the wrong ones. Let me run out to my truck. I'll be back in a jiffy."

"It's really hopping around here this morning," Grant said after the painter left the room. "Do they always keep you this busy?"

"No," Kelli began, "this is—"

"Miss Harrison?" Larry strode in, his tool belt jingling at his waist. "We got us a problem. Can you come down for a minute?"

Grant sighed in frustration. Kelli shrugged apologetically and escaped to the kitchen.

Larry gestured toward a large hallway closet just off the kitchen, intended for the washer and dryer. He opened a blueprint. "The doors for this closet are out in my truck, but the print calls for—"

"There you are," interrupted the painter, panting with exertion as he entered the room. "I just went upstairs looking for you."

From the living room behind them, there began a loud hammering. Then the ear-splitting screech of a table saw rent the air.

The painter leaned closer. "I've got two different paint companies here," he shouted, opening two brochures and spreading them out on the counter, "both top quality.

Which color white do you want?"

Kelli glanced at the brochures. Each paint company offered fifteen different shades of white. "I need to look these over in natural light." She took the brochures and moved to the window, where she stared at the small, colored squares.

Navajo White. Cloud White. White White. Eggshell. Ivory. Alabaster. Swiss Coffee. Which one would look the most neutral?

The hammering on the other side of the wall increased in intensity, seeming to echo through the floorboards. *Bam, bam, bam!* With each blow Kelli found herself blinking involuntarily.

Someone nudged her. It was one of the younger carpenters. What was his name? He wore a red sweatshirt and was opening a blueprint.

"Sorry to interrupt, but this calls for three shelves in that built-in bookcase in the dining room," he said loudly. "Do you want the shelves permanent or adjustable?"

"I don't know," Kelli said. She was about to study the print, when Larry reached over her shoulder and covered the blueprint with his own. To her relief the sawing and hammering stopped at the same instant.

"Hold off on the shelves a minute," Larry said. "I need a decision on these closet doors. The print calls for louvered doors. Don't know if somebody made a mistake, but the doors I've got with me are solid. If I have to take them back and order new doors I need to know now."

"Just a minute." Kelli desperately tried to keep her cool. "Let me take things one at a time."

"Excuse me, miss?" The painter moved closer,

nervously scratching his head. "I realize you're busy, but these gentlemen will be here for a while, and I've got an appointment in Carson City this morning. If you could just take a quick look at those paint chips, I'd appreciate it."

"Take a number, buddy," Grant called out.

He stood behind her, his back against the opposite counter, his arms crossed as if he'd been watching and listening for some time.

Larry snatched the print from Kelli and turned to Grant. "Do you know anything about these doors?"

"How long will it take to order louvered ones?" Grant asked.

"A couple of weeks."

"Order them." Grant gently lifted the paint brochure out of Kelli's hands and glanced it over. "Eggshell," he told the painter.

"Good choice." The painter scribbled on his clipboard.

"Wait a minute," Kelli cried. "I didn't—"

"Sign here and I'll be out of your hair." The painter extended the clipboard to her.

Stubbornly, Kelli grabbed the paint brochure and turned her back on the two men. Eggshell *was* a nice, neutral shade, she had to admit. A good compromise between white and off-white. Probably the same one she would have chosen. Kyle and Desiree would like it. But still ....

"I'll sign," Grant said.

"You can't—" Kelli began, wheeling around, but the painter was already grinning appreciatively as Grant scribbled his signature. He gave Grant his card, said he'd be back on Wednesday, and hurried out.

Grant took Red Shirt aside, issued a few instructions, and consulted again with Larry. The table saw started up again, rising in volume right along with Kelli's temper.

How dare Grant start handing out orders, as if he owned the place? How dare he sign that form? She wasn't some little, fainthearted maiden in distress.

To her further indignation, he headed for the stairs, gesturing for her to join him. When they reached the studio and shut the door, blocking out much of the noise, she whirled on him furiously.

"What do you think you were doing down there?"

"Helping you."

"I don't need your help. This isn't your house, Grant. The men report to me. I was handling the situation just fine."

"I saw how fine you were doing. The minute that saw started you went into a catatonic trance."

"I did not."

"You would have been down there all day at the rate you were going."

"I would not have taken all day! I just needed a few minutes to think. I want to make sure I'm making decisions Kyle would approve of. I have a responsibility to keep this house on schedule, and to do it right."

"I know that. But you have a responsibility to keep *our* work on schedule too."

"I told you it wasn't going to be easy, working here."

"It *can* be easy, if you'll just let it." He shook his head with rising frustration. "My entire reputation is at stake on this presentation. If you spend too much time worrying over every little detail on this house, we'll never get finished. Hell, we'll never even get started!"

"Details are important. I'm sorry if I don't make decisions fast enough for you. And I didn't appreciate you taking over the reins like that."

"I was just trying to speed things up." He heaved an exasperated sigh and sat down at his stool. After a moment he added carefully, "Look, Kelli, we've got a lot of work to do. Can we bury our weapons for the rest of the day? Call a truce? We'll get a lot more done if we're not at war."

Fuming, Kelli took her place at the drafting table without another word. Bury her weapons, indeed. She wasn't being unreasonable. He was. He hadn't even said he was sorry. How could she ever have imagined she was attracted to this man?

But as they plunged into their work, there was so much to do, and so many creative problems to solve, that her irritation over the way Grant had usurped her authority with the workmen was soon forgotten.

He was quick and highly inventive. Despite their poor start, they soon began operating as partners, with the give and take and constructive criticism that made for a successful creative session.

The carpenters continued their labors without interrupting them further, and a brief check reassured Kelli that they were moving forward according to plan.

By the end of the day, she and Grant had thumbnails for most of the collateral materials—small-scale layouts she'd have to work up into full-size comps—and they had agreed on two possible color schemes. They also had three new logos sketched out.

They didn't like any of them.

"Let's dump the Alpine theme," Grant said. "Try a completely new look. A logo that's really different."

"Sure. Instead of pine trees, how about palm trees?" she kidded.

"Palm trees," Grant mused, trying to look deeply serious. "Great idea."

"We center the name *Cassera's* between the sun and the surf. Add a grass hut. A few sweet-and-sour spareribs."

"They can redo the interior of the casino to match. Indoor waterfalls. Barmaids in leis and sarongs. As for the ad campaign ...." He sketched something, then showed it to her: a cartoon of a grinning pineapple on snow skis, wearing a lei and grass skirt, and shaking a pair of dice. Above it, the headline: *Hula for Moola.*

She couldn't help laughing. "That's pretty good. I thought you said you didn't do illustrations."

"I said it wasn't my specialty." He tossed the sketch pad aside and looked at her. "We made a lot of progress today. More than I expected."

"It did go pretty well. All things considered."

He turned to her with a contrite smile. "About this morning … I probably overstepped my bounds with the workmen. The house is your territory."

Her lips curved into a wry grin. "Is that an apology?"

"It is. I'm sorry."

"Apology accepted."

"I'll try not to let it happen again." He stood up, took her hand in his, and kissed it. The soft touch zinged up her arm, sending her heart into a skid. "How about having dinner with me?"

The invitation caught her off guard. She'd managed to get through a day with Grant on a purely platonic, professional level. But was it wise to spend the evening with him as well?

Before she could protest, he'd leaned a hand on her drafting table, bent down, and was staring directly into her eyes.

"You've got to eat, Kelli. And I just happen to know this little Italian place with food you've got to taste to believe."

"Italian?" Her favorite.

He grinned. "I'll go to my hotel and change. Be back for you in about an hour?"

CHAPTER 5

"I found this place a couple of years ago," Grant said. "Now I come up here every time I'm in the area."

"How often is that?" Kelli asked.

"Every chance I get."

The restaurant was warm and cheerful, with a fire crackling in the hearth, red-and-white-checked cloths on the tables, and clusters of grapes entwined in trellises overhead. When they arrived, the waiter had greeted Grant like an old friend and led them immediately to a secluded booth.

"They make the world's best veal Marsala," Grant said, touching his fingers to his lips. "Just like Mama used to make."

Kelli smiled and sipped her cocktail. "Are you saying that literally? Was your mother a good cook?"

"The best. Her grandmother was from Italy, and a real tyrant, from what I'm told. They say I got my temper from her, and my stubborn streak from my father's side of the family."

"Are they Italian, too?"

"No. Welsh."

Of course, Kelli thought. Welsh. That explained Grant's dark good looks and blue, blue eyes. And it explained, too, his strength of character, his determination to succeed, and the stormy side of his personality she'd seen surface on occasion. Inherited from ancestors who'd had to fight hard every day for survival.

"My great-grandfather came from a little fishing town on the southwest tip of Wales. He emigrated to America when he was fifteen."

"Our ancestors had a lot in common. My grandfather came over when he was twelve. From Ireland."

"An Irish lassie. So that's where you got your devastating wit, the fiery hint of red in your hair. And your—" He broke off.

"Your fiery temper?" she put in, gently teasing. "Wanted to add that, didn't you?"

His eyes twinkled. "Your words, not mine."

"But you thought it."

He grinned at her across the table and gave his shoulders a little shrug. "So, we both have a temper. So what? It's just one of many things we have in common. We're both creative types. We have the same gutsy approach to life. We seem to have a lot of the same tastes and interests. That's a good thing."

"Is it? Maybe we're too much alike. Maybe that's why— as you put it—we were at war this morning."

Grant shook his head. His voice dropped a decibel or two. "There's no such thing as 'too much alike.' That's an old wives' tale." Some new emotion flared brightly in his eyes as he studied her.

Kelli looked away, his expression causing her heart to pump in an odd rhythm. You're *not* out on a date, she reminded herself. Grant is temporarily your boss. *This is just a business dinner.*

The waiter rescued her from further distracting thoughts by arriving with antipasto salads for each of them. Being served without ordering was a new experience for Kelli. She looked at Grant in surprise.

"No menus?"

"Veal Marsala isn't on the menu. I had to call ahead of time to order it. I couldn't let you leave Tahoe without trying it. And what's an Italian meal without antipasto salad and minestrone soup?"

She forced a smile and said nothing. It was nice of him to arrange all this in advance for her enjoyment, but she was also a bit annoyed. He was keeping the upper hand again, not allowing her any say in what they did.

What if she didn't like veal, or his choice of soup or salad? She might have preferred something else on the menu.

The waiter smoothly withdrew the cork from a bottle of wine. Kelli saw it was a Cabernet Sauvignon. She opened her mouth to protest, then thought better of it. Once Grant had approved his sample taste, the waiter moved to fill Kelli's glass.

"None for me, thank you."

"You don't drink wine?" Grant asked.

"Not red wine. I'm allergic to it."

"Allergic?"

"It's too high in ... I forget what it's called, but it's something in the grapes' skins, that gives the wine its color. I love *white* wine. And I adore champagne. But ...." She shrugged apologetically.

"You should have said something."

"You didn't ask."

He fell silent, blushing slightly. "You're right. I should have asked. Let me order you something else. How about a white Zinfandel? Chenin Blanc?"

"No, please, don't bother. I couldn't drink a whole bottle. I'm fine."

He frowned. She could see he wasn't pleased with himself. "Not allergic to veal, I hope?"

"Nope."

He blew out a relieved breath.

The salad and soup were truly excellent. When their dinner arrived—veal smothered in a sauce of mushrooms, wine, and onions—Kelli inhaled its rich aroma, took a bite, and pronounced it delicious.

"Batting 500, anyway." Grant sipped his wine and eyed her thoughtfully. "I'm sorry about the wine. And for ordering ahead of time."

"It's okay."

"No, it's not. I should have checked with you first." He sighed. "I'm beginning to think I've been my own boss for too long. I'm used to handing out directives, making instant decisions without consulting anyone. That's the only way a business can operate sometimes. When something matters to me, my instinct is to plan it out, make arrangements in advance, so things will run more smoothly."

He laughed softly, in self-reproach. "But I can see the instinct doesn't work *quite* so well away from the office. Lately, even my brother and sister have been telling me to lay off."

"Lay off what?"

"I have this tendency to jump in whenever either of them has a problem, to try to fix things, make things easier for them. When Glen lost his job last month, I set up three job interviews for him. He was annoyed, told me to mind my own business." Grant shrugged. "They used to turn to me for help and advice all the time, but now—"

"*Turn* to you for advice? Are you sure? Or were you handing it out unsolicited?"

He looked at her in surprise. "I don't know. Maybe I was. There's five years between me and Glen, and my sister's two years younger than he is. I've been through so many things, when I see them about to make some of the same mistakes I've made, I can't help—" He paused. "Did I really say that? I sounded exactly like my father."

"My father, too." Kelli laughed. "And my four sisters."

"Counting your brother, six kids?" His eyes widened and he whistled. "Wow, that's some family."

She nodded. "I'm the youngest. When I was born, I think they all got together and decided, hey, this scrawny kid is never going to make it without our help. So, they took me under their collective wings. Every time I turned around, they were telling me how to dress, how to talk, what classes to take, where to go, who to go out with. I went along with it because I looked up to them. Finally, I realized I wasn't living my own life. I was pleasing everyone but myself."

"So, you said, forget this. From now on, I'm my own boss? Is that why you quit your job at T & M?"

"Yes. I loved it there at first. But then they brought in a new creative director. He was always looking over my shoulder, afraid I'd come up with something better than he did. When I managed to sneak through ideas of my own that met with approval, he took credit for them himself."

"What an idiot. A wealth of talent at his fingertips and he was afraid to use it."

"It was a good learning experience. I won't let it happen again."

"The other day, you compared me to your last boyfriend. What did you call him?"

"Mr. My-Way-or-the-Highway. It's a name my brother came up with. Wayne had definite opinions on everything. The way he saw it, he was always right. When I look back on the time I was with him, I feel like I just disappeared."

"I'm sorry."

"It wasn't all bad. He was a wonderful man in so many other ways. He just believed that he knew what was best for me. He had this way of joking about it. He'd say 'Babe, when I want your opinion, I'll give it to you.' After a while, I didn't find it funny anymore."

"No wonder you were so reluctant to work with me when I showed up here with the whole thing sewn up. And no wonder you bit my head off this morning over that mess with the workmen." He sighed. "I'm surprised you didn't get up and leave when the waiter brought the wine."

"I'm glad you finally understand."

He leaned forward on the table. "*I'm* glad you explained all this. I'll do my best to watch it from now on. I won't plan anything or do anything that affects the two of us without consulting you first. Okay?"

Kelli held back a smile. "I have a feeling that's easier said than done."

"Maybe. But I'm going to give it a try." He paused. "And I'm going to ask you for something in return."

"Oh?"

"There's something I want you to do. Even if you're not particularly wild about the idea, will you agree to try it once, for my sake?"

She looked at him. "I assume this *something* is strictly business-related?"

His lips twitched as he considered the question. "In a manner of speaking."

There's a hidden motive here, she thought. But what? Cautiously, she said: "Okay. To quote you: I'll give it a try."

"Great. What do you say we head down to the casino and play blackjack?"

THE DEALER'S name tag read *Sean*. He grinned at Kelli as he shuffled the cards and presented them to her.

"Cut?"

Kelli smiled back, trying not to be nervous as she divided the deck in half. Grant had refreshed her memory on the rules of the game as they drove down.

"Why don't *you* play?" she'd asked when they arrived.

But Grant had insisted that she take the open spot on the stool. He wanted her to win back the money she'd lost the first day, and he wanted her to do it herself. He was just there to help if she needed it.

There were three other players. The heavyset man sitting on the stool next to her was named George. Kelli placed two dollars, the table's minimum bet, inside the small, white circle in front of her. Sean dealt.

Grant moved up behind her, resting one hand on the padded edge of the table beside her. Although their bodies weren't touching, she felt the heat radiating off of him and from his cheek so close to her own. Her pulse moved into high gear.

"Grant," she whispered sternly, hoping he'd take the hint and move away. He didn't budge.

"Relax," he whispered, his breath warm against her ear. "This is strictly research. You want to win, don't you?"

She took a deep breath and picked up her cards, struggling to will away her awareness of him as a man. *As if that were humanly possible.*

Her hand totaled thirteen. She saw the dealer's up card: a two.

"Stand," Grant said in a low voice.

She glanced at him. "Stand? On a thirteen?" He nodded silently.

She needed twenty-one to win. She'd never stood on anything as low as thirteen. She flicked her cards against the felt tabletop to indicate a hit.

The dealer turned up a nine. Disappointed, Kelli laid down her cards. "Bust."

The dealer also went bust. Two of the other players

collected their winnings. Kelli felt a prickle of disappointment. If she'd stood pat, as Grant had insisted, she would have won, too. But there was no way Grant could have known the dealer would go bust. Was there?

She played another hand and won. On the third hand, Grant murmured another direction against her ear. It seemed less sensible than the first.

"I know you're trying to help, but I'd rather play it my way," she said firmly.

She lost.

"You're one stubborn lady. I'm offering free advice. You ought to take it."

"I like to make my own decisions. I know how to play."

"You promised, if I asked you to do something, you'd try it. I'm asking now. Follow my advice."

She sighed. "All right. But just this once."

On the next deal she held two sevens. The dealer's up card was a king. A tricky hand to play. She looked at Grant.

"Hit," he said. She asked for a hit. She reached nineteen, and the dealer went bust. Kelli grinned.

"Now don't get cocky, just because you were right this once."

But she soon noticed that Grant's eyes were fixed in concentration on every card that was played. It occurred to her that he was using a system. She had no idea how a system worked, but as his advice continued to work, her excitement grew.

Grant moved up even closer behind her now, until the warm strength of his body rested against her back. "You're doing great," he whispered softly, his lips against her hair.

His nearness distracted her and disturbed her senses,

sending shivers dancing through her. She kept on playing, hardly aware of what she was doing, relying completely on Grant's directions.

Grant encouraged her to up her bet. When an hour had passed, she'd won more than twice as many hands as she'd lost and had stacks of chips in front of her.

"You've brought me good luck, pretty lady," one of the other players said, gathering up his winnings. "I'm gonna quit now while I'm ahead."

"How much have we won?" Kelli asked.

Grant made a quick mental calculation. "About three hundred dollars."

She had no idea it was so much. "Shouldn't we quit now, too?"

"Not quite yet."

"Hit?" the dealer asked.

Kelli's eyes darted to the table. She hadn't even realized he'd dealt. A fifty-dollar bet stood inside her circle. When had she put it there? It was too late to take it back. Heart pumping with alarm, she picked up her hand. She had an ace and a ten. Blackjack!

Both thrilled and relieved, she reached out to collect her winnings. Grant stopped her hand. "We'll let it ride."

She stared at him. Let it ride? A hundred and twenty-five dollars? She was about to protest, but Grant silenced her with a look.

"Trust me," he said. "This time, it's double or nothing."

George, who'd been about to leave, sat back down on his stool. "I've got to see this."

Kelli's stomach felt queasy. She picked up her cards.

Over a hundred dollars. It was crazy to bet so much on one hand. Then she caught her breath. A king and a queen! Twenty points; almost a blackjack.

"Stand," she said. The dealer had a six and an ace; soft seventeen. He had to take a hit. Kelli's heart began to pound. She watched him turn up an eight. The ace could count for one, so he now had a total of fifteen.

The dealer paused before turning over his next card. Kelli wondered where all the air in the room had gone. Grant squeezed her arm, and she felt a bond of camaraderie pass between them in that moment of tense excitement, of shared danger.

The dealer turned over his card. A jack. He'd gone bust.

"We won!" Kelli stood up and threw her arms around Grant's neck, laughing in delight.

Grant responded immediately, capturing her around the waist and grinning. "I told you we would. It doesn't hurt to let someone else take the lead once in a while, does it?"

Looking up at his lips just inches away, Kelli's face flushed with sudden color at her spontaneous hug and she started to pull away. He wouldn't allow it.

"Nothing like it, is there?" he said softly.

"No," she whispered, unsure if he meant the act of winning or the feel of their embrace. "There isn't."

Kelli felt high as a kite. She could walk on water. She could float on air. Altogether they'd won more than five hundred dollars. The thrill was so great she felt as if they'd won the Irish sweepstakes.

"I couldn't believe it," she said later, as they drove back

to the house, "when I saw that fifty-dollar bet. Did I really put it out there?"

"No. I did."

"I thought so." She slapped his thigh. "That was sneaky."

"Somebody had to place the bet. You didn't seem to be paying much attention to the game for a while there."

How could I, she thought silently, with you standing so close behind me? "I was paying attention. Enough to know you were using some kind of system. What do you do? Count cards?"

"It's a bit more complicated than that."

"Explain it to me."

He spent the rest of the drive going over the theory he'd studied and had practiced over the years. There was a whole series of rules, but it basically involved keeping a count of the cards that had been played and keeping in mind the ratio of face cards to non-face cards that were left in the deck. He raised or lowered his bet according to the odds.

"Does it always work?" she asked.

"No. It can work spectacularly, as you saw tonight. But when it fails, it fails dismally."

"And you told me to trust you! What if we'd lost that last bet?"

"We would have lost," he said simply. "But I knew the deck was heavy on face cards at that point. The odds were well weighted in our favor. It was worth the risk."

It was nearly midnight when they reached the house. He walked her to the front door and followed her in, shutting the door behind him against the cold.

"Thank you for coming tonight," he said. "It was fun."

"It was. I'm glad I came. And thank you for dinner. It was delicious."

"Have you forgiven me yet for ordering ahead of time?"

"I have."

Their eyes met in a warm smile. He didn't say anything for a while, just stood a few feet away, watching her, his eyes brimming with affection. She found her mind straying to the way his body had felt, pressed against hers, as she had struggled to keep her mind on the game.

Wanting to brush away such thoughts and fill the silence, she cleared her throat and said: "Well. It's late. I have to get some sleep. The guy I'm working with thinks 6:30 A.M. is a fine time to start."

"Slave driver. I'll have to talk to him."

"Please do. Tell him I was up late doing research. Ask him if we can start at a more civilized hour tomorrow. Like maybe seven-thirty?"

"I'll see what I can do."

"Well ... good night." It seemed ridiculous to shake his hand yet again, so she kept her arms at her sides.

"What?" he asked in mock chagrin. "You're not going to invite me to stay for a cognac and a fireside chat on your couch?"

"No cognac. No fire. No couch."

"We'll have to make do without, then." His arms glided around her so naturally it seemed as if she were made to fit within them. Her tiny, surprised intake of breath was lost as, suddenly, his lips were on hers.

He kissed her softly, slowly, a feather-light touch that aroused her instantly. She knew she should tell him to stop, but she couldn't. Beneath her skin, she was quivering. Heat spread through her. She could barely think.

She gave in, let her mind go, forgetting everything but him, his delicious scent and taste, the way his body felt against hers. Her hands went up around his neck and she closed her eyes. One hand caressed the strength of his broad shoulders, the other tangled in his hair. It felt soft and silky, just as she imagined it would.

Her body melted against his. His mouth moved so slowly, so tenderly over hers. If he took as much time, she thought, with the rest of her body as he did with his kisses, he'd make a wonderful lover.

A wonderful lover.

The three words invaded her thought processes, and her mind slowly began to clear. What was she doing? How could she allow herself to respond to him like this?

She ended the kiss and gently pushed out of his arms, her heart beating wildly.

"Kelli—" he began, his voice deep and rough.

"Please. Just give me a minute." She took a few shaky steps toward the living room and stopped to look out the windows, trying to still her rapid breathing, waiting for the wave of desire to fade.

The inky silhouettes of the pine branches outside framed a brilliant crystal moon in a midnight sky. Below, a glowing moonlit path crossed the surface of the lake, fading to darkness just before it reached the shore. A sight for lovers, she thought, smiling grimly at the irony. But we aren't lovers. We can't be.

"We can't do this," she said at last. She heard him move closer.

"Do what? Kiss?"

"We can't get involved. You said yourself, it's not a good idea to mix business with pleasure."

"I said I *used* to think that. Since I met you, I've changed my mind. I think you know I've been attracted to you from the start."

She turned to face him, struggling to maintain her resolve, hoping he couldn't see that she felt exactly the same way. "We'll do far better work if we just stay friends and colleagues."

"I disagree."

"Haven't you seen what happens in office romances? The two people are so caught up in each other that their work suffers. They can't concentrate on the job. Worse yet, if anything goes wrong between them, it disrupts the entire working environment."

"We're not working in an office, Kelli. It's just the two of us. Nothing we do can affect anyone else."

"But it will affect *us.* As you pointed out yesterday, there's a lot at stake here. This account is big and important. We've got less than two weeks to do a major presentation. A relationship between us will only get in the way."

His eyes locked with hers, rife with emotion. He sighed heavily. "You're probably right." He reached up to gently touch her cheek with his fingertips. "It's not going to be easy, given the way I feel about you. But I guess we can be professional about this. And keep our hands off each other until the job's finished."

Until the job's finished.

What then? she wondered. The pleasant bantering they'd shared over the past few days swept through her mind. The joy she felt in his company. The pleasure of talking with him over dinner. The magnetic attraction that sizzled between them. The melting effect of his embrace. Even now, the light touch of his fingers against her skin was rearranging her breathing patterns.

A few days ago, she'd been certain she didn't want to get involved with anyone for a long, long time. Now that she'd met Grant, she wasn't quite so sure.

Then she remembered the part of his personality that clashed strongly with hers: his instinct to hand out directives, to make arrangements in advance, unasked. Tonight, he'd resolved to consult her before making future decisions. But she doubted he could alter a part of himself that was so deeply ingrained.

Why did she always seem to fall for men who were overbearing and dictatorial? Wayne had always promised to change, but he never did. If she let herself get involved with Grant, Kelli realized, she'd be stepping right back into the same, self-destructive pattern. She'd simply disappear.

"Grant. Please don't take this the wrong way." She forced herself to continue, feeling her resolve slipping even as she uttered the words aloud. "But I don't expect this ... relationship ... to turn into anything else down the road."

For a second he seemed to reject what she was saying. Then disappointment took over his face. He jerked his hand back, his lips tightening as he struggled to compose his features into a mask of calm, polite indifference. "Okay. I get it."

He opened the front door. "I'll see you in the morning at eight. I hope that's a civilized enough hour for you." And then he was gone.

~

IT WAS A GOOD THING, Kelli thought the next day, that they'd done most of their creative planning the day before, because now Grant barely spoke a word to her.

While she worked steadily on pencil comps for menus and brochures, he spent a good part of the day on the phone, giving his production manager details so he could get prices from printers.

The little talking that they did was strictly related to the project at hand. Grant was pleasant and businesslike. He still approved of her work in general. But it seemed to Kelli that he was more critical today, and his comments were less constructive.

"I don't like it," he said late that afternoon, when she presented him with a new logo idea.

"What's wrong with it?"

"The typeface is too ornate. I want something clean and bold."

"Is there anything you like about the concept?"

"No."

She worked up three more designs, all different. He studied them with narrowed eyes. "I like the mountain in this one, and the typeface over here. Try doing one that combines the two."

"I think they work fine as they are," she said defensively. "Let's show them all to Ted and see what he thinks."

"I'm not going to show Ted ten different logos. It'll take his board a year to make a choice. We'll come up with one that we like, maybe a runner-up, and that's it."

"But there's no way this combination will work. It's a waste of—"

"Try it," he replied curtly.

"You're just making me do this because of last night. You want to get back at me for—"

"This has nothing to do with last night."

"Doesn't it? Then why have you been in such a bad mood all day? Acting so distant and standoffish?"

"I thought that's the way you wanted it."

"You know it's not. I said I didn't want to get personally involved. I just want a professional, working relationship."

"Well, this is the working relationship you got. Take it or leave it."

Holding her temper in check, Kelli sat back down at her table. Clearly, he was taking her resolve as a rejection. Why couldn't he understand how she felt? She'd tried to explain it to him. Why did he have to be so picky? Why did he think his ideas were best?

Just keep going, she told herself. Stay composed. Be competent. This job will look great on your resume. When it's finished, you'll be back to working for yourself, with all the creative freedom you want.

When she completed the new drawing according to Grant's directive, she sat back and studied it. It was a graphic representation of a rugged, snowy mountain-top, with the name *Cassera's Tahoe* superimposed across the bottom in bold, outline-style letters.

To her surprise, it wasn't bad. In fact, she had to admit, it was better than the originals she'd done on her own. The more she looked at it, the more she liked it.

"Hey," Grant said, looking over her shoulder. "Great

job. That's what I'm looking for. The shape is really interesting. It'll lend itself to all the different pieces. And it's easily recognizable, easy to read." A grin spread across his face for the first time that day. "Everything about it is just right. That's *it.*"

Kelli was hugely pleased, felt the tension in the air recede. Since the result was due to their combined efforts, she reasoned that she owed him an apology.

"You were right. I shouldn't have objected when you told me to try it this way. I'm sorry."

He sat on the stool next to her and picked up a pencil, rolled it between his fingers. "I'm the one who should be apologizing. I didn't want to hear what you told me last night. And I've been acting like a teenager with a bruised ego all day. I'm sorry. Is there a chance we can forget what happened, and get back to square one?"

"I'll forget it if you will," she said with relief, wanting more than anything to restore peace between them.

He didn't reply, only smiled. After a while he got up, opened the studio door, and listened to the silence. "Carpenters gone?"

"They finished a couple of hours ago. The painters start tomorrow."

"If there's one thing I can't stand, it's the smell of wet paint." He slowly crossed the room, musing. "What do you say we get out of here tomorrow and do something fun?"

"Really? You think we can afford to take a day off?"

"I think we've *earned* a day off. We've put in two long days and got an outstanding amount of work done. We've got plenty of time left."

"Twist my arm."

He laughed. "What would you like to do?"

"You're asking me? You're the Tahoe expert."

"And if you were anybody else, I'd walk out this door, plan the whole thing myself, and spring it on you in the morning. But I took notes at the dinner table the other night. Tell me what *you* want. Anything goes."

"Anything?"

"Anything."

"Let me think." She was about to suggest they go skiing, when her gaze drifted to the lake view beyond the bay window. "How about a boat ride on the lake?" she said impulsively.

His eyebrows lifted. "A boat ride? In December?"

"I've cruised the Seattle harbor. And I've sailed bays and lakes all across Washington State. But I've never been out on Lake Tahoe. It's so beautiful. I'd love to go out on the water, see the view of the shoreline from the middle of the lake. I guess it'd be pretty cold out there, though?"

"Freezing."

"Do they even rent boats this time of year?"

"No."

"Oh. Well, you said *anything goes*. So. If I could really do anything that I wanted ... I'd love to go boating."

He chuckled to himself. "Just for the fun of it, what kind of boat did you have in mind?"

"A powerboat. Something fast."

She saw the familiar gleam in his eyes that meant he was plotting something. He slapped his hand against the table and grinned. "If a boat ride is what the lady wants, a boat ride is what the lady gets. I'll be here tomorrow about ten. Dress warm."

"Should I pack a picnic lunch?"

"I'll take care of it." He stopped halfway to the door. "Maybe I should ask ... is there anything else you're allergic to?"

"Peanut butter."

"Then rest easy tonight. I won't serve PBJs."

CHAPTER 6

Kelli leaned on the railing above the private dock, admiring the craft below, water lapping quietly against its white hull.

She'd never ridden in a powerboat quite so big or so sporty and luxurious.

It was huge—at least twenty-eight feet long, she guessed. Navy and red stripes raced its length at deck level, and waist-high metal railings skirted the top of the V-shaped bow.

Most boats were in storage this time of year, Grant had explained during the short drive to Logan Shoal. Lucky for her, an old friend of his family was on the sheriffs' posse and kept his personal inboard/outboard ready to go all year long. It had a radar wing, tilted up and backward like an enormous handle over the rear of the cockpit.

"I really appreciate this," she heard Grant say. He came out of the nearby boathouse with a man of about her father's age. She went to meet them by the steps, where Grant introduced them.

"Thanks so much for letting us use the boat, John," Kelli said.

"You're most welcome." The lines in John's face deepened as he broke into a wide smile. "On second thought, maybe I'll take this lady out on the lake myself," he added with a wink.

"Don't even think about it," Grant growled.

John slapped Grant on the back. "Don't worry. It takes a younger man than me to go out on the lake for pleasure this time of year. Too cold for my bones."

"At least we have a good day for it," Grant pointed out. "Clear sky. Not much wind."

"True." John turned to Kelli. "I don't lend my craft out to many people, but I never could say no to Grant. I think by now he handles a boat better than I do. Care to guess how long I've known this young whipper-snapper?"

"Since long before he had so much snap in his whip, I'll bet." Kelli laughed.

No wonder Grant hadn't been stymied when she asked to go for a boat ride in the dead of winter. He was an experienced sailor. And he had connections. She was struck with the realization of how much she had to learn about him. And the fact that, with each passing day, she was discovering more and more interests they had in common.

The two men hopped onto the deck and Grant reached out a hand to Kelli, helping her climb on board. The cockpit, high atop the boat behind a tilted windshield, took up the back third of the boat and was fitted with padded benches. The instrument panel held as many dials and gauges as a small aircraft.

While Grant stowed a picnic hamper in the quarters

below deck, John opened a storage locker and handed her the flotation cushions that substituted for life vests.

"Grant's family's been coming up here since he was about three, maybe four. We used to rent them our guest house down the road. What a little daredevil he was, jumping in and out of my boat. He kept begging me to let him drive. Finally, I taught him the ropes. When he grew up, every girl within fifteen miles was dying to go out on the lake with him."

Despite herself, Kelli felt a stab of jealousy. "So, Grant's taken a lot of girls out on the lake?"

John's lips twitched as he looked at her. "Oh, you know these hot-blooded young guys."

Before Kelli could respond, Grant reappeared on deck. "What am I missing?"

Kelli shot him an accusing look. "John was just telling me what a *hot-blooded* young guy you were."

"John, are you spreading lies?"

John chuckled. "Wipe that scowl off your face, young lady. I'm just teasing. Take my word for it, you've got yourself a great fellow here. If I could have had a son, he's the one I'd choose."

He clapped an affectionate hand on Grant's shoulder, then jumped back onto the dock and knelt to loosen the tie line. "Now you two have yourselves a good time. I'm not on call today, so you can keep her out as long as you want."

Grant stood at the helm and waved to John. Kelli sank into the curving bench across from the helm and crossed her arms, glancing at Grant with feigned indignation. "What a relief to find out I'm spending the day with an *experienced* man of the sea. Every girl within fifteen miles was dying to go out on the lake with you, huh?"

Grant looked surprised beneath his grin. "Is that what he told you?" He cupped his hands over his mouth and shouted, "Thanks a lot, John! Good to know I can always count on a buddy like you!"

"Anytime!" John saluted from the dock.

"Is it true?" Kelli asked.

"Not jealous, are you?"

"No! I just like to have an idea of who I'm dealing with."

"It's not true." Grant adjusted two levers on the instrument panel and glanced her way, his eyes deeply serious. "It was just every girl within five miles."

Stifling a laugh, Kelli bent forward menacingly. Grant held up an arm to ward off her blow as he turned over the ignition. The sound of their laughter disappeared beneath the engine's roar.

He guided the boat out of the stone breakwater to the choppier water of the lake, where he relaxed against the wide helm seat, one hand on the controls, the other at the wheel.

"I thought we'd head north, around the lake," Grant said. "Let you see how big it really is. That is, if you're still speaking to me."

She let her wry smile answer in confirmation.

Kelli zipped up her ski jacket against the chilly air. As they moved past the dense thicket of pines along the shoreline, the loud hum of the engine kept their conversation to a minimum. After a while she spotted her brother's house, almost hidden by the trees.

Along the northern shore they passed Mount Rose, a

majestic peak beyond snow-covered pines. At Crystal Bay, Grant cut the engine. She saw another boat far in the distance, but otherwise they were alone.

"Let me know if you get too cold and want to go back," Grant said.

Kelli shook her head. "I love it out here."

He seemed pleased that she was enjoying herself. "Me too. I wish I had more time to go boating. I'd buy one of these for myself and dock it at San Francisco Bay."

"Why don't you have time?"

He shrugged. "I practically live at the agency. This is the first time I've been away in two years. Even though we've been working up till now, it's felt like a vacation to me."

"You ought to get away more often. You have to make time for the things you love. Hasn't the place been running okay while you've been gone?"

"As a matter of fact, it has." He leaned back and stretched out his legs, clasping his hands behind his head. "You're right. Let's not even think about work today."

Kelli sat back, hands in her pockets, her face tilted up toward the sun. They drifted in delicious silence for a while. The lake stretched endlessly around them in gleaming sapphire-blue splendor, and the sky above matched its brilliant hue.

WHEN THE SUN was high in the sky, Grant said it was time to start thinking about finding a place for lunch.

"I read about a famous bay that's supposed to be really beautiful," Kelli commented.

"Emerald Bay?"

"That's it! Can we go there?"

"We can. But it's at the opposite end of the lake."

"Is that too far?"

"Depends on how hungry you are."

"How fast does this thing go?"

"I usually keep it at thirty or forty knots. It planes at forty-five."

"Let's go to Emerald Bay. And let's plane it."

Grant grinned. "Your wish is my command." He moved the throttle slowly forward.

Kelli watched the shoreline recede as the boat picked up speed. Soon the trees blended into a dark-green blur stretching up to the snow-covered mountains above. The boat beat against the cresting water before them, vibrating powerfully with the engine's hum.

She stood up, bracing herself against the windshield for support, squinting against the cold slap of wind that roared in her ears and blew her hair out behind her like a flag. And then, suddenly, the boat stilled, skimming across the water as if they'd left a runway and had truly taken off into the air.

Wonderful, she thought exultantly, drinking in the clean taste and smell of the crisp, fresh air. *Magnificent!*

Cheeks glowing, she ducked behind the protective windshield and sat down again. They broke into laughter at the same moment, lost in the pure joy of movement, sight, and sound.

When he'd slowed the pace to a safer speed, Grant slid to the far side of the double-width helm seat and gestured toward the waiting space. "Want to drive?"

Kelli's lips parted in astonishment. She'd never driven a

boat before. Her first impulse was to say no. But then she saw the challenge in his eyes, which brought to mind a similar challenge she'd accepted not too long ago, to briefly take over the controls of her brother's small plane over Puget Sound. *That* had been thrilling.

"Sure," Kelli replied, her pulse quickening with excitement as she moved behind the wheel. "Just tell me what to do."

He showed her how to move the throttle to change the speed, and pointed out Mount Tallac, a lofty white peak far in the distance. "That's our guide. Keep it at eleven o'clock and we'll end up at the mouth of the bay."

It proved easier to pilot the boat than she'd expected, and her anxiety soon vanished in the thrill of the ride.

When they reached the other side of the lake, with Grant's direction she found the narrow opening in the trees that led to a lovely, oval-shaped bay. A small island was nestled in its protective shelter. Around them, tree-covered cliffs rose up sharply from a narrow strip of rocky beach.

"A poet couldn't do justice to this view," Kelli enthused.

Grant reached across her to cut the engine. "This is probably the most photographed spot in the whole area."

She watched him climb, swift and surefooted, to the bow of the boat to drop anchor. With his dark hair blowing in the breeze, his jeans clinging to his long legs, and the black ski jacket that fit snugly across his shoulders, he was the epitome of masculinity: Tall. Handsome. And utterly desirable.

She gave her head a shake. *Wrong. He's your boss on this*

project. You work for him. And, as you so clearly stated the other night, that's as far as this is going to go.

When Grant returned, she pointed to a turreted stone castle on the nearby shore and asked, "Does anyone live there?"

"No. That's Vikingsholm Mansion, a replica of a ninth-century Norse fortress built by an heiress in 1928. The property is now part of the Emerald Bay State Park. I'll have to take you there when the tours start again this summer."

She let out a regretful sigh. "I'd love to see it. But this summer, hopefully, I'll be knee-deep in work back in Seattle. I don't know if I'll have time to come down."

"You ought to get away more often," he said softly. "You have to make time for the things you love."

The gleam in his eyes and the way he'd echoed her earlier words disconcerted her. She felt a shiver dance down her spine and knew it wasn't from the chilly air.

She tried to look at something neutral—the instrument panel in front of him or the back of the seat—but her stare kept drifting back to the sheen of his hair, the way sunlight reflected on his smooth-shaven cheek, the inviting curve of his lips.

She stood up abruptly. "You wouldn't believe how hungry I am. How about if I go grab the lunch?"

Grant told her she'd find a box lunch in the refrigerator. Kelli pushed through the narrow folding door to the cabin. It was warmer below deck, and its cozy sophistication delighted her at once. Floor space was limited, but there was plenty of headroom.

On one side was a compact dinette booth upholstered

in blue velveteen. The galley opposite boasted a gleaming stainless-steel sink and stove below teak cabinetry. At the bow of the boat was a luxurious double berth, and when she turned, she found a matching berth at the stern. The dinette probably opened into a bed, too.

Cozy, she thought again. Enough sleeping space for six.

Sleeping space.

The thought made her heart race. To prevent any distracting images from coming to mind, she quickly opened the tiny refrigerator. Its contents made her start in surprise.

Stuffed in one corner was a cardboard box with a deli label and two stemmed glasses. Around it, the shelves were piled high with more than a dozen bottles of wine. What were they all for?

She pulled one out: Sauvignon Blanc. She pulled out another: Chenin Blanc, from one of her favorite Napa vineyards. There were three different Chardonnays. A Gewurztraminer. Riesling. Zinfandel. All from different wineries. And every one of them white.

There were also two bottles of very fine champagne: Krug and Dom Pérignon.

Her heart warmed at Grant's thoughtfulness. She put the cardboard box into the picnic basket he'd brought, added the bottle of Chenin Blanc, the Dom Pérignon, and the glasses, and brought it all up on deck.

"You really know how to spoil a girl." She gave Grant a grateful smile as she set the basket on the cockpit floor.

He smiled back. "You said white. And you said you adored champagne. I didn't know what kind you liked best. Did I hit the mark with any of them?"

"The bull's-eye." She handed him the bottles and the corkscrew. "I've been known to kill for a glass of either of these."

He laughed. "So have I. Shall we start with the Chenin Blanc?" At her nod, he expertly opened the bottle and filled the glasses. "Here's to ..." He paused, seeming to change his mind about what he was going to say, before finishing: "... a winning presentation for Cassera's."

~

"TELL me about all the girls you used to take out on John's boat."

Lunch had been scrumptious. Cold, fried chicken, fresh fruit, potato chips, French rolls with butter, and moist, chewy brownies for dessert.

They'd been deep in conversation when a freezing wind had come up, so they'd escaped to the warmth of the cabin below, where they now relaxed side by side at the dinette table, sipping delicious champagne.

"You really want to hear about that?"

"I'm intrigued by a man who—as you so blithely stated —has gone out with every girl within five miles."

Grant laughed and shook his head. "You know I was pulling your leg. So was John. I think he's a bit envious that I brought you out here today. I told him we're working together—that this is just a business arrangement. He seemed inclined to think otherwise."

Grant sipped his champagne, catching her gaze, his expression suggesting that his hopes were more in line with those of his friend.

Kelli blushed under Grant's scrutiny, unable to deny that—despite her resolve the other night—she'd been harboring similar thoughts about him which were anything but businesslike. "You're avoiding my question," she blurted out.

"Am I?"

"Yes."

"It's good for business colleagues to share aspects of their personal lives, in order get to know each other better."

"Okay." His voice seemed to lower an octave. He set down his glass, slid one arm behind her along back of the dinette seat, and turned to face her. "My dating history. I'm not seeing anyone now. My last serious relationship ended over a year ago. I've dated a number of women over the years. Everyone plays the field. Don't you?"

"Not really."

"No?"

"The men I went out with—either it ended after one date or it lasted a long time."

When had he moved so close? Grant's thigh, hard and lean beneath his jeans, now pressed against hers, trapping her between his body and the wall of the boat.

"The ones that lasted a long time ... were there many?" he asked quietly.

"Just two."

"I take it the second, long-lasting relationship was Wayne?"

She nodded. The admiring look in his blue eyes caused her pulse to pound. "When we broke up, I promised myself

I would fly solo for a while. Not get involved with anyone. Until ...."

"Until what?"

His face was just inches from hers, his lips so close ... so incredibly close. Her nerve endings started a frenzied rain dance, and her fingers began to tremble, prompting her to set her champagne glass down on the table.

"Until I'd found out if I could survive on my own, answer to no one, become my own person."

"You are definitely your own person, Kelli Ann Harrison." Grant's fingers closed over hers. "Every day I discover something new and even more remarkable about you. You're a beautiful, strong, ambitious, talented woman. Any goal you set for yourself, anything you want to achieve, you'll do it. You've got what it takes."

"I hope that's true." Her voice was little more than a whisper.

His hand slipped into her hair, and then he bent his head and brushed her cheek with a brief kiss, as gentle as the touch of a butterfly's wings. "Believe me, it *is* true."

Kelli gripped the table edge to steady herself against the tremor that ran through her at his touch. He drew back slightly, a silent question in his eyes as they held hers for a long, heart-stopping moment.

She'd said she didn't want this. She'd tried to resist. But she saw in his expression such heartfelt tenderness that it stripped away her defenses. She didn't want to think, only wanted to feel.

Her eyes must have mirrored both her yearning and her change of resolve, because his arms suddenly tightened about her with confidence and his lips came down on hers in a deep, clinging kiss.

He kissed her as she'd dreamed of being kissed by him —open-mouthed, drinking her in.

He tasted of champagne. His delicious scent filled her, surrounded her. His hands caressed her back, pressing the softness of her sweater against her sensitized flesh. When the kiss was over, she gazed up at him, her vision desire-misted, and she saw open affection in his eyes.

He now pressed kisses across her cheeks, nose, and throat. Her eyes closed in rapt absorption as he moved aside the soft cowl neckline of her sweater to expose her neck. She breathed in long, deep waves, enjoying the moment. After what seemed to her a pleasurable eternity, his lips once more reached her waiting mouth.

There was no need to speak. They were communicating their feelings and thoughts now through touch and silent gesture. Their lips met and parted and met again, liquid, searching. Her fingers combed through his soft, wind-blown hair and she drew him closer still.

Her breath came faster as his lips and tongue found her most sensitive spot at the side of her throat. His hand slipped beneath her sweater, brushing the side of her breast.

The feeling she had of wanting him to touch the tips of her breasts was so strong that her head fell back, and she let out a small, yearning sound.

"Ah, Kelli," he murmured.

She felt his strong arms around her back, drawing her forward, up, and out of the booth. Then he was carrying her, settling her gently onto expansive softness. She was hazily aware that he'd brought her to the bed, and she felt light and dreamy, waiting heedlessly for what was to come.

She felt a sensation of movement beneath her, of the world gently rocking, and wondered at it. Then he was beside her and she forgot everything as he tugged at the hem of her sweater, pulling it up and over her head.

She gasped when his hand closed over one of her breasts, massaging it through the thin lacy fabric of her bra. His mouth moved slowly over her collarbone and down, and then he was kissing the upper curve of her breasts. She moaned unconsciously, tiny, violent explosions echoing through her body.

He moved above her, melding his mouth to hers once more as he covered her body with his. His lips and legs pressed her into the soft mattress, infusing her with his warmth.

She was vaguely aware of an increase in the movement beneath her, a rhythmic rolling, back and forth—what did it mean? His hand covered her breast again, molding it with palm and fingertips.

She was spinning, lost in the pleasure of his hands and mouth. It felt so right to be in his arms, to have him touching her this way. She wanted to feel his flesh against hers, wanted him to make love to her, wanted him as she'd never wanted anyone before.

Suddenly the world jerked sharply, heaving them to one side. His weight hurtled against her and she clung to him, eyes widening in surprise, her mind still reeling on some distant plane. Then the boat tilted back again, and they rolled with it. He hugged her tightly and spoke softly in her ear.

"It's all right, Kelli. We're anchored down. We're not going anywhere."

She tried to control her breathing and the pounding of her heart. "Is it a storm?"

He shook his head. Softly, with affection, he touched his nose to hers. "It's just a wave. The wind."

"How do you know?"

"There was hardly a cloud in the sky today."

Anxiety filled her. They were so far from shore. "Don't you think we should check?"

He raised himself above her with a sigh. "If it will make you feel better, I'll go and check."

He rolled out of the bed and moved to the cabin door. The loss of contact with his body sent a chill running through her. She rolled to her side, all at once uncomfortably aware of her state of undress as the boat continued its gentle rocking.

"Just a strong wind." Grant dropped back into the cabin. "We've got a few whitecaps, but nothing to worry about." He slid back onto the bed and stretched out beside her. "Now, where were we?" Tenderly his arms gathered her up and he lowered his mouth to hers.

Her heart hammered in her chest and she tried desperately to let her mind drift back to where it had been only moments ago. But now, for some reason, she kept hearing his voice saying *Everyone plays the field. Don't you?*

She'd never made love to a man she wasn't in love with. She'd known Grant less than a week. In that short time, she'd come to—how should she put it?—to like him intensely.

She deeply enjoyed his company. She felt close to him

after all the hours they'd spent together. She'd felt a magnetic, physical attraction to him from the moment they met. That's what had brought them together now.

But that wasn't love.

She'd felt certain, after his kiss the other night, that any further physical contact would lead to this very dilemma. Now she saw she'd been right.

How could she face him tomorrow, the next day, the next week, working together in the close confines of the house, knowing she'd had casual sex with him? What would he think of her? What would she think of herself?

He felt her tension, sensed the difference in her response, and he pulled back, searching her face. "What's wrong?"

"I ...." she began. But she couldn't put her feelings into words. She felt his eyes on her face and couldn't look up. Her cheeks flushed with guilt and confusion.

He sat up. With a deep, steadying breath, he found her sweater and handed it to her. Swiftly moving off the bed, he grabbed his jacket and went to the door.

"Come up when you're ready," he said, and to her relief there was no trace of anger in his voice. "We'll head back."

A few minutes later she climbed up on deck. It seemed ironic that the sky was still such a bright blue, and the distant pines and snowy mountains were still so breath-taking in their magnificence, when inside she felt as if she'd withered up and died.

Grant sat at an angle across the helm seats, long legs stretched in front of him, his hands in the pockets of his jacket. The wind blew briskly through his hair and whipped her own hair about her face, but otherwise it was silent.

She sat opposite him and made herself look at him, but his gaze was focused downward, avoiding hers.

"I'm sorry," she said.

"It's all right. Don't worry about it." He lifted his eyes to hers. She saw no accusation there, only self-reproach and frustration. "You made it clear the other night how you wanted things to stand between us, and you repeated those feelings today. I overstepped my bounds, that's all."

"It wasn't your fault." Tears stung her eyes. She wanted to say, *I wanted it just as much as you did,* but the words wouldn't come.

"It was." Grant toyed with the keys in his hand. "I just want you to know, I didn't bring you out here for this—as a pretext to make love to you. I promised myself last night that I'd play by your rules. That I could think of you as no more than a colleague and business partner. I see now that I was lying to myself.

"You must have known—there's no way I can hide it— from the moment we first bumped into each other in front of that elevator, I've been crazy about you. And today ... I couldn't help myself. I just got carried away." He let out a deep sigh. "I'm sorry. It won't happen again."

The ride back to the dock seemed interminable. Grant barely said a word. Kelli told herself she'd done the right thing. She ought to be relieved that they hadn't made love, instead of feeling this irrational disappointment that ached, hollow, inside her.

Don't think about it. Don't think.

They returned the boat, got into Grant's van, and drove

back to the house. When he pulled into the driveway and stilled the motor, he sat back, tapping his fingers on the steering wheel.

She was trying not to imagine what the next few days were going to be like, how she should act, when Grant spoke.

"I'm going back to the city tomorrow morning."

"Tomorrow?" Her eyes darted up to his, but the dismay that rang in her voice embarrassed her and she looked away.

"I have meetings with clients on Friday. I was going to have to go back tomorrow night in any case."

She knew why he was leaving early. After what had happened, he felt just as uncomfortable as she did. "When will you be back?"

"Saturday, if everything's going smoothly at the agency. You don't need me here for a couple of days, anyway. We've got the logo design. You just need to work up a tight comp. All the thumbnails are done for the collaterals. You can do the full-size comps on your own. When I get back, we'll start on the media campaign. We'll have almost a week left, plenty of time."

She nodded, afraid to speak because her throat had suddenly, inexplicably constricted and she felt the hot threat of tears.

He looked at her, hands still on the wheel. "Will you be all right while I'm gone?"

She nodded.

"You'll call if you have any questions?"

She nodded again.

"Good." There was a silence. "So. Do you have your key?"

She realized he was signaling for her to go. She fumbled for her purse and threw open the door. "Have a good trip. See you Saturday," she said. But her lips wouldn't smile.

"See ya." He turned on the ignition, backed up, and drove away.

CHAPTER 7

Kelli's eyelids grew heavy. The drawing blurred. She sat up, arching her neck and back, and checked her watch under the glare of the lamp above her drafting table: 3:00 A.M., Friday.

She'd been working since nine the previous morning, with only short breaks for food and fresh air. No wonder waves of sleep were lapping at her. No wonder her entire body ached.

Pushing herself up from the drafting table, she switched off the overhead lamp and made her way to the bathroom. The painters had finished that morning and fortunately the smell of paint was beginning to dissipate. She got ready for bed, then opened the bedroom window a crack. A rush of cold air surged in, and she breathed deeply.

She was about to move away when a soft, whispering sound made her pause and look outside. Through the darkness the pine branches looked thicker and heavier than before, and tiny specks seemed to be drifting softly through the air.

Snow! A light fall of beautiful, delicate flakes. She'd been working so hard, she hadn't even noticed it start.

Fresh powder on the mountain, she thought, with a small burst of excitement. She hadn't scheduled any workmen for the next day, since she wanted to give the paint a few days to dry before the carpet was laid. She was almost done with the work Grant had left for her. At last, she could get out for a day and go skiing.

Grant. Shivering, she slipped into her sleeping bag and pulled her blankets over her, then curled into a ball and hugged one of her pillows to her chest, waiting for her body heat to generate warmth.

She tried to lull herself back to sleep with images of the next day's activity—a glorious day out on the mountain—but she kept seeing Grant's face before her, lined with hurt and self-reproach. She kept hearing him say, *I'm sorry. I couldn't help myself. It won't happen again.*

Grant. She wondered how many times she'd whispered his name in the day and a half since he'd been gone. The first night she'd tossed and turned, her mind tormenting her with memories of his kisses, of the way his hands and lips had felt on her body, of the desire he'd awakened within her when he held her in his arms.

At last, near dawn, she'd fallen into a heavy sleep, only to awaken, hot and highly aroused, from a dream that had moved rapidly from romantic to erotic and had featured Grant as the lead.

Today she'd worked frantically to make the hours pass more quickly, but it hadn't helped to banish thoughts of Grant or to ease the pang of loneliness and longing she felt each time she looked up and saw the empty drafting table beside her.

She missed him. And not just his embraces. She missed his company. Their teasing banter, their meaningful conversations, his smile, his ready laugh, his keen interest in her and everything she said.

How could she feel such attachment to someone she'd known only a week? Kelli realized now that the day on the boat, when they were on the verge of making love, the attraction *hadn't* been merely physical. At least, not on her part.

I shouldn't be surprised, she thought. Relationship experts and cautionary friends often insisted that it took months, sometimes years, of sharing and caring before a person could truly say they were in love with someone.

But her own family history had taught her otherwise. Ever since she was a child, she'd been told by her parents and grandparents—whose relationships she had as living proof—that it was entirely possible to fall in love overnight, and for that love to last a lifetime.

She hadn't really believed that something so magical would ever happen to *her*. But she couldn't deny it any longer: the magnetic pull she'd felt when she and Grant first met had grown into something far deeper and richer in a very short time.

With a certainty that filled her with equal measures of joy and confusion, Kelli admitted that she was falling in love with him. That she might be *in love* with him already.

What was she supposed to do with all these newfound feelings? Could she tell him? No. Not yet. It was much too soon.

The timing, she knew, was all wrong. She'd meant it when she said she wanted to stay single for a while, to prove that she could be happy and make it on her own. How was she supposed to do that, if she got involved with Grant?

It still worried her that he had such a forceful personality. At times, the two of them were like gasoline and flame. All it took was a spark to ignite their tempers. They were too much alike, and something told her they'd always be fighting each other to retain control.

But none of that seemed important anymore.

She had no idea where this would lead, or what the future might hold for them. It might be a very short-lived affair. But he clearly had feelings for her. He wanted to be lovers *now*.

Admittedly, so did she.

She'd been afraid that a romantic liaison would hamper their working relationship, but she saw now that by denying them the chance to express their feelings for each other, she'd only put up a barrier between them that would become more difficult to cross with each passing day.

Who knows, she thought; maybe an affair would actually be good for us. He'll be my muse, and I can be his. Hopefully, we'll bring out the best in each other.

Her heart pounded with excitement as she thought of the days ahead. She'd have to let him know that she'd changed her mind, that she *did* want him. But when? How? He was due back the day after tomorrow.

I'll tell him soon, she decided.

Somehow, she'd know when the time was right.

~

"ARE YOU KIDDING ME?" Kelli scooped up a fistful of snow, formed it into a ball, and threw it against a nearby pine in frustration. "I don't believe this!"

The sky was still a threatening gray, but the snow had stopped falling at nine A.M., so she'd cleared her car windows and strapped her skis to the roof rack. A four-inch layer of snow covered the long, sloping driveway that led to the main road, but it was still navigable as long as she put chains on her tires. After an hour of struggling, she'd finally managed to attach them.

But just as she'd climbed behind the wheel, the engine had died. The situation under the hood told a familiar story: it was the automatic enrichment device again. She had hoped the earlier repair would last her another few weeks at least.

If she had four sets of hands, she could get it working again, but she knew it would just be another Band-Aid. What she needed was a new part. And she'd never find one in Tahoe. She'd be lucky if she found one anywhere in the state.

There were no Rover dealers in America anymore. Unless a specialty shop happened to have the part in stock, she'd have to order it directly from England, and that would take weeks, maybe months to get.

"It's not fair!" Scooping up another snowball, she turned and threw it down the driveway with all her might.

"Hey!"

She saw him at the same moment that she heard his

deep shout. He came to an abrupt halt about twenty feet away, one arm raised to protect his face.

"Are you through, or should I start arming myself?"

"Grant!" Her heart gave a leap of delight and she ran to meet him.

"Who did you think I was? The county building inspector? A bill collector?"

"Neither. I didn't even see you."

"A likely story." He brushed the splatter of snow from his parka and quickened his pace in her direction, his boots making deep footprints in the soft snow. Beneath his open jacket she saw that he wore the familiar jeans that accentuated the lean, muscular strength of his thighs and calves.

She stopped close to him, curbing an almost desperate need to throw her arms around his neck and hug him. She'd been worried, after what happened on the boat the last time they were together, that he'd feel awkward and uncomfortable around her.

To her relief, she saw no trace of discomfort in his gaze. If anything, she detected warmth in his eyes as he looked at her, a mirror of the joy she felt at seeing him. Although his smile was reserved, as if he were holding himself in check.

"I thought you had meetings with clients today," she said. "You weren't coming back until tomorrow."

"I heard on the news that you had snow up here. I was afraid you might be snowed in."

"You missed your meetings just to make sure I was all right?"

"I did. Shameful, isn't it? I shirked my responsibility and sent someone else. I had images of you stuck out here alone with an impassable driveway, and six-foot drifts piled up against your door. So, I loaded my van with enough food and supplies to last for a month's siege and beat it up here. I figured I'd hire a sleigh and a team of huskies if I had to pack it all in."

She laughed. "It would have been a daring rescue. I'm sorry I missed it." This proof of his feelings for her was both flattering and thrilling. She grinned shyly. "You know, you could have called."

"I did. Your phone's out of order."

"It is?" she replied in surprise. "It has been quiet, but I wasn't expecting any calls. And I never used the phone."

"The snow probably weighed down and broke the line. It's common this time of year. It can take days to fix."

"Well, thank you for coming." She wanted to tell him how lonely it had been without him, how much she'd missed him. *Not yet. Not yet.* "Where'd you park?"

"At the side of the road. They were just clearing it when I got here, so I didn't bother to put on chains. I couldn't risk that snowy driveway of yours, though." He took in her outfit—royal blue bib ski overalls with a white sweater. "Were you going skiing?"

"I *hoped* to. I need a break. I'm almost finished with the comps for the collaterals. Only two left."

"Are you serious? You must have worked all night!"

"Actually, I did."

"Then you *definitely* deserve a break." He glanced at her car. "What's wrong? Did it die again?"

She nodded. "Same old problem. The A.E.D."

"Then you're in luck. I brought a new part with me."

"An A.E.D.? For this model Rover?"

"Yep."

"You're kidding." Kelli stared at him. "How on earth did you get it?"

"I looked in the right place. I didn't want you stranded here." He moved past her and slammed down her hood. "We can install it tomorrow."

"That was so thoughtful, Grant. Thank you so much! But I still don't see how you—"

"Heavenly Valley has a foot of new snow," he interrupted, unhooking her skis from her roof. "I've got my ski equipment in the van. Let's unload the food I brought, I'll glance over the work you did, and then what do you say we go hit the slopes?"

SHE COULD SEE why it was called Heavenly Valley. Standing at the top of the mountain, surrounded by puffy white clouds in a bright-blue sky, with the warm sun beating down on her face, Kelli felt as if she truly had reached the heavens.

Miles below, past the long expanse of frosty white mountainside, beyond the snow and pine-covered valley, the lake spread itself out like a shimmering mirror, echoing the blue of the sky.

Even from this height, the lake seemed enormous, curving toward them in a giant arc and then disappearing around a bend in both directions. The opposite bank appeared only as a hazy mass of white and green, like a distant, massive island.

She grasped her ski poles with gloved hands and leaned forward, stretching her legs and arching her back, catlike, to counter the effect of the long ride up the mountain on two separate chair lifts.

Grant kick-stopped at her side. "Nice view."

"It's beautiful!" Kelli took a deep breath of the crisp, sparkling air.

"I wasn't talking about the lake." His eyes twinkled as he took her in, seemingly admiring Kelli's slim form.

She blushed, both flattered and embarrassed. She was wearing her favorite ski outfit, a royal blue jacket with matching sweater and overalls, and a black faux fur hat pulled low over her forehead and ears.

"I can see why you love it here so much."

Grant stamped his skis, shaking off a thin layer of snow. "We can take Ridge Run first, if you want." With his pole he pointed out a gentle slope along the top edge of the mountain. "It's the easiest, and you can see the lake all the way down."

He'd asked, on the way up on the chair lift, how well she skied. In fact, she'd been skiing since she was three years old, but some attempt at modesty—or maybe it was a mischievous instinct—had made her shrug and say simply, "I've hit the slopes a few times."

Grant shoved off and slipped past her. "Just take it easy," he called out over his shoulder. "I'll wait for you at the first bend."

Smiling to herself, Kelli followed him down the long, curving trail, enjoying the feel of the smooth, freshly packed snow beneath her skis and the crisp wind against her face. It was Friday, and the slopes weren't overly crowded.

Grant's black bib ski pants and parka stood out in sharp

relief against the backdrop of pure white. He moved with expertise and precision, his skis perfectly parallel, slowing almost imperceptibly before each turn and then picking up speed again in a fluid, graceful motion. An expert, Kelli thought. Why hadn't she thought to ask how long *he'd* been skiing?

He stopped at the side cresting the next ridge, hands resting on his ski poles, looking up at her. She could almost feel the heat of his gaze as she finished the slope with quick, even turns and slid to a stop, her skis just inches from his.

"You ski like a pro," he said.

She tried to hide a smile. "So do you."

He shook his head in disbelief. "Here I've been taking it easy, and you could go down this thing backward with a blindfold. What were you sandbagging for?"

"I wanted to surprise you."

"It worked." He grinned as two other skiers zoomed past them. "And it's the nicest surprise I've had all day."

The morning passed in a rush of shared laughter and vibrant energy. At lunchtime they huddled over hot coffee and sizzling hamburgers in the noisy, steamy cafeteria, then attacked the slopes again, delighting in their matched abilities.

When the clouds gathered, graying the sky, and the wind turned cold, they agreed to take just one more run before tackling the lower slopes that led to the parking lot.

"I'll race you." Kelli pointed to a sign classifying a nearby slope as most difficult. "Last one to reach the line at Waterfall Chair has to cook dinner."

"A serious challenge. Don't you have to throw down a gauntlet?"

She pulled off a glove and tossed it at his feet. "Will that do?"

"Admirably." He bent to pick up the glove and handed it back. "Ready?"

She nodded. They pushed off. Kelli sped down the mountain, snow flying, her breathing increasing with her rate of speed. The slope was so steep it was nearly deserted, and she was glad. It was not going to be easy to beat him, she saw, when they were three-quarters of the way down.

Grant was still keeping pace with her, now a few feet ahead, then behind. She zoomed around a high mogul and forged to the front in a burst of speed. Moments later she heard a victorious cry as he sailed past her through open air, then landed smoothly a good dozen feet beyond.

He jumped the mogul I avoided, she thought. She should have tried it. But then, to her horror, she saw him waver on his skis, lose his balance, and fall. He rolled over himself in a tangle of snow, skis, and poles, finally sliding to a halt at the far side of the hill beneath a tall tree.

"Grant!" Kelli screamed.

Her chest tightened with fear as she sped down the slope to his side. His skis had disengaged and come to a stop in the snow a few feet above. He lay limply on his back, his eyes closed, his hat gone, snow in his hair.

Awkwardly, still wearing her skis, she knelt down in the soft, unpacked snow and leaned over his prostrate form. Half-choked with fear, she reached out to touch his cheek.

He grabbed her, pulling her down on top of him,

knocking the breath out of her in the impact against his chest.

"Cheater!" She tried to squirm out of his arms but failed. She lay across his chest, gulping great breaths of air, her legs twisted behind at a crazy angle, her face close to his.

He grinned up at her, infuriatingly pleased with himself. Annoyance replaced fear and then both dissipated in a shaky laugh. *Thank God you're all right*, she thought.

She said: "That was a rotten thing to do."

"What? Taking advantage of a perfectly good ski jump to gain some ground? Or nearly killing myself?"

"You know what I meant. Playing possum."

"Simple revenge. You sandbagged. I played possum."

"I thought you were hurt!" She impaled him with a good-natured glare. "You owe me an apology. I was terrified."

"Were you?"

"Yes!"

"Then I *am* sorry." His voice was suddenly quiet. He brushed a stray lock of hair from her forehead. Her pulse quickened, and, lying on his chest, their faces nearly touching, she imagined she could feel his heart pounding through the layers of their clothing.

She wanted his kiss so much she trembled, but she could see from the hesitation in his eyes that he was holding himself back. Afraid to say aloud how she felt, she tried to tell him with her eyes. Then she lowered her mouth to press against his.

She heard his sharp intake of breath, and then his arms tightened around her and he met her kiss with unrestrained passion. A tight knot loosened within her and desire flowed through her. Her hands slipped around his neck, wet with snow. She knew they were meant to kiss each other like this, meant to be in each other's arms.

"Grant," she whispered, and was about to say, *I want you so much. I was wrong before.* But just then a spray of snow hit the back of her neck and she jerked up with a start.

The icy coldness slid down inside the collar of her jacket and sweater. She shuddered and cried out, quickly shaking out the snow, wanting to shout something obscene at the skier who'd sent the offending blast and who now swooshed past them. Instead, she caught Grant's eyes, and they both burst out laughing.

He sat up, took off her hat, and freed it of snow. He ran his fingers through her tangled hair, smoothing it, then replaced her hat on her head. Hesitantly she turned toward him, wondering if he'd read the message in her eyes. But the intensity of the previous moment had gone.

"Ah," he said, shaking snow out of his hair, "the joys of the great outdoors."

"No respect. Absolutely no respect."

He stood and flexed his legs. "Well, they still work."

She sidestepped up the hill, retrieved his skis and poles, and brought them to him.

"Thanks. I guess you're going to ask for a rematch."

"No way. I've had enough racing for one day. It's late, anyway, and I don't like the look of those clouds. Let's go home."

"You've talked me into it. Only one problem. How will we know who's supposed to cook dinner?"

"Easy. You've been disqualified on two counts. One:

unauthorized use of ski jump. Two: failure to finish the race. You lose."

He was still putting on his skis. "But you didn't finish the race either."

With a grin, she shoved off and headed down the mountain. "I will now."

~

"I won a contest on the back of a cereal box."

"You're joking."

"I'm serious," Grant said. "That's what got me interested in advertising."

They sat over dinner in the living room at a folding table covered with a white cloth, china, silverware, and glowing candles that he'd brought from home. A fire blazed and crackled in the hearth beside them, casting waves of light and shadow across Grant's face. In the hushed room, Kelli felt the same tense excitement she'd felt all day on the slopes.

When they'd returned to the house, she'd offered Grant the use of the shower downstairs. After her own shower and a change of clothes, she'd found him in the kitchen, whistling as he chopped vegetables for salad, while the microwave defrosted a container of his own homemade spaghetti sauce.

He was dressed in a cashmere sweater and jeans, his hair glistening-wet and clean. The urge to slip up behind him and wrap her arms around his waist had been so strong she'd had to turn away and steady herself against the counter.

Looking at him now, across the table by candlelight, she felt the same warm rush of desire. She wondered what he was thinking and feeling, and what might happen between them later that night. He said he'd checked into a motel that morning. She wanted him to spend the night here, with her.

But after everything she'd said and done, how and when should she let him know that she'd changed her mind?

"The cereal's advertising mascot was a tiger," Grant was saying, "and he needed a name. I entered the contest and won."

Kelli willed her heartbeat to slow down as she twirled her last bite of spaghetti around her fork. "You named a tiger on a nationally advertised product? Pretty good. What did you call him?"

"Grrrrr-egory."

She laughed. "That's great! How old were you?"

"Nine."

"A child prodigy! Your parents must have been proud. What did you win?"

"A free trip for two to Madison Avenue, New York, to tour the ad agency that handled the account. I was so impressed. Plush, plush, plush. They treated me like visiting royalty. I was suckered in on the spot."

"And you vowed at that moment to have your own ad agency someday."

"Something like that."

He stood up and they cleared the table. Standing side by side at the sink, they washed the dishes by hand.

"What about you?" he asked. "What got you interested in this crazy business?"

"I just like to draw and paint. I always have. My mom enrolled me in art lessons when I was in fifth grade, and before long it became my passion. When I realized that a person could actually earn a living as an artist, I was over the moon. It's a good thing it worked out, because my back-up profession—at least the one I imagined in child-hood—was to be a chef."

"A chef?"

She nodded, smiling. "I thought cooking would be glamorous. As it turns out, I'm hopeless in the kitchen."

"No kidding? Someone as creative as you?" He dried his hands on a towel and leaned on the counter. His hand rested just inches from hers. She wanted to touch it.

"I could never make a spaghetti sauce like yours—it was delicious. My mind is always somewhere else. I forget ingredients, I leave it on the stove or in the oven too long, something gets burned ... I guess I don't have the patience to cook. All that effort, and the food disappears in an instant. At least when I do a painting or a sketch, I have something lasting to show for my efforts."

"I enjoy cooking. I find it relaxing. After the pressures and decisions at the office all day, breaking my neck to solve conflicts and please clients, it's a treat to come home and whip up something to suit just my own taste."

"I'm glad you feel that way. At least one person in this relationship ought to be good at—" She broke off, heat rising to her face.

His eyes met hers, and she saw a tangle of emotions

there—surprise, puzzlement, desire, doubt. He started to speak, then stopped himself.

Kelli groped for words. *Say something. Tell him how you feel. Tell him you were wrong before, that you want him.*

The words didn't come.

His lips tightened and he moved to the kitchen window. "It's snowing again."

Disappointment surged through her. She took a shaky breath. "I thought it wasn't supposed to snow until tomorrow."

"So said the weatherman."

"He probably used that blackjack system of yours to make his prediction. When it works, it can be spectacular, but when it fails ...."

He didn't smile. Why were they standing here talking about the weather? Her heart beat like a drum. In the quiet room she was aware of his presence with such force that her skin felt his touch even though he was half a dozen feet away.

"I guess I'd better get going."

She tried to hide her dismay. "Already?"

"If I wait too long, I'll have to put chains on."

"Oh."

He went to the window again. "I was going to say—you might think about getting out of here yourself, so you don't get snowed in. But I guess it's okay. It still looks pretty light out there."

"Like last night," she offered.

He nodded, hands in his pockets.

The tension was so thick in the air, it crackled.

She took a deep breath, forcing the words out. "You

could ... stay here if you like. I wouldn't mind. I know there aren't any beds, but I have a sleeping bag and lots of blankets."

A long silence fell. He lowered his gaze. She blushed furiously, desperately embarrassed, unable to look at him. Did it mean he was no longer interested?

After a moment he said quietly, "I don't think so. But thanks." She heard him move to the kitchen door. "And thanks for the skiing today. It was terrific."

"Yes. It was." She stared at the floor, her pulse beating wildly, her eyes burning.

"Well, goodnight."

"Goodnight."

She heard the front door close with a final, agonizing click. The tears she'd been holding back sprang into her eyes. She snapped off the kitchen light and stumbled up the stairs in the darkness, clutching the rail.

She stubbed her toe on the top step and cried out, flicked on the hall light, splashing a diffused glow across the floor of the master bedroom. In spite of the studio equipment filling one side, the room had never seemed so huge or so empty until that moment.

In the corner where she slept, Kelli dropped to her knees on the blankets that lay across her sleeping bag and took a deep, choking breath.

A footstep sounded on the stairs. Her mind spun with confusion and she turned, rising shakily to her feet. Grant stood in the open doorway, his eyes finding hers across the softly lit room. She tried to find her voice but couldn't.

Hesitation warred with desire within her, and even

halfway across the room she saw the same turmoil reflected in his gaze.

"The snow is coming down harder now. I don't think you should—"

"Grant." Tears welled once more in her eyes. Barely above a whisper, she added, "Please. Stay with me tonight. I want you to."

As if her words had released him, he was suddenly beside her, his arms catching her up, enfolding her in his embrace. And then his lips were covering her face with kisses, and finally, urgently, melding with her own lips.

With gratitude, pleasure, and relief, her hands wrapped around his waist, holding him close, the way she'd longed to hold him all day. She buried her face in the softness of his sweater, then pressed kisses across the whisker-roughened skin on his neck and cheeks.

His mouth came to hers again, and then, gazes locked, they undressed each other, taking their time because they knew, now, that nothing would stop them.

The room should have felt cold, but she was warm, flushed. They touched the skin they bared with wonder and delight, as if discovering a treasure that was theirs and theirs alone.

His smile was radiant as he looked at her slender body, his eyes telling her he found her beautiful. He smoothed his hands across her skin, felt the softness of her breasts, the curve at her waist. She touched trembling fingers to his chest, through the dark curling hairs, where she felt his heart beating wildly against her palm.

Gently, her hand in his, he pulled her down beside him atop the blankets, cold at first touch and then warm as her body molded to the heat of his. He gathered her into his arms, her softness curving against the lean, hard muscles of his arms and stomach and legs.

Her hands glided down the length of his back, over his firm buttocks and back up again, delighting in the smoothness of his skin. He covered her neck and shoulders with soft kisses, every touch setting her flesh tingling, and she felt his arousal, which added fuel to the flames that already raged within her.

"Kelli ...."

His hands moved slowly across her body, gently molding her breasts and their sensitive peaks. His lips followed where his hands had been, and he took into his mouth first one breast and then the other.

She wanted to hurry, hurry, an urgency building within her at each touch of his hands and lips. She moaned when his fingers traveled the length of her body, then found the warm, pliant flesh that ached for his touch. She was on fire, everywhere, wanting him, needing him to fill the void he'd created.

He moved on top of her. Driven by the passion they'd both held back for so long, he joined his body with hers. She moved against him, pulling him closer still, his flesh hot against hers.

With each thrusting rhythm he took her higher, soaring until she shuddered on the very brink of ecstasy. It's never been like this, she thought, and then she let herself go, releasing her mind to the bright light of sensation.

It seemed they were one being, a perfect melding of souls, nothing left but feeling and the joy of discovery they saw in each other's eyes.

~

A PATCH of light spilled across the floor, bathing their bodies in its reflected glow. Kelli's arms were wrapped around the smoothness of Grant's back, wanting to prolong the peaceful feeling of sharing with him, the sensation of naked flesh against naked flesh as they lay clasped together.

"I wonder," Grant whispered in her ear, "what this will do to your theory."

"What theory?"

"The one that says we'll do far better work if we just stay friends."

She laughed softly. "Well, I had trouble concentrating before. It can't be any worse now."

He raised himself up on one elbow, looking at her. "You had trouble concentrating?"

She nodded.

"I thought I was the only one. You'd be sitting there, sketching away, deep in thought, so beautiful, so close ... and yet so far away. I couldn't keep my eyes off you. I wanted so badly to take you in my arms. But I knew once I'd done that, there'd be no stopping."

"I felt the same way."

"I can see us now. We won't be able to work five minutes without a break."

"But the work we get done in that five minutes will be brilliant. Inspired."

"No doubt." His fingertips trailed across her shoulder, then slid down to cup her breast. All at once she shivered, aware that she was covered with gooseflesh.

"I think my toes are numb."

"So is my backside." He kissed her. "What do you suggest we do about it?"

"We could open up the sleeping bag, lay it flat, and crawl under the blankets."

"An excellent idea."

A few minutes later, snuggled under the blankets and wrapped in each other's arms, he murmured, "Good advance planning."

"What?"

"Bringing two pillows."

"I always sleep with two pillows."

"Why?"

"One for my head. One to hug."

"You hug your pillow?"

"Every night."

"What for?"

"I don't know. I guess I feel more ... secure, if I've got something to hug."

He rolled back on top of her, eyes shining in the moonlight. "Tonight," he whispered, "you'll have all the security you need."

To Kelli, the night passed as if in a dream. In Grant's loving embrace, she felt truly, completely alive for the first time in her life. He brought her to a peak of brilliant awareness, a joyful surrendering, a pleasure unlike any she'd ever imagined.

Afterward they talked, getting to know each other more fully as they shared their personal histories and revealed intimate details of their lives.

Intermittently she slept. Tender visions filled her

dreams, from which she'd rise through heavy, swirling darkness to find Grant's hands and mouth gently loving her into wakefulness, and then, almost without moving, he was inside her, making them one.

At dawn, Kelli awoke in Grant's arms, their legs entwined, her cheek warm against his chest. She felt his heartbeat, heard the soft brush of the wind and the tap, tap, tap of pine branches against the house.

Grant stirred and opened his eyes. "Morning, beautiful."

"Morning."

Lifting her head, she squinted against the soft morning light. Beyond the window it was a blur of white. She gave a little gasp.

"I think we have ourselves a blizzard."

CHAPTER 8

"A blizzard?" He rose from their makeshift bed and went to the window, unheedful of his nakedness. "Wow. It's a beauty of one. Man, it's freezing out here."

Quickly, he grabbed both their sweaters from where they lay on the floor and slipped back under the blankets, shivering. Pulling his sweater over his head, he encouraged Kelli to do the same. "About a foot and a half of new snow and still falling hard," he said when they were snuggled once more in each other's arms.

"Does this mean," Kelli asked lazily and without regret, "we're going to be snowed in?"

"Not going to be. Already are. Unless you want to hike out, we're not going anywhere today."

"What a shame." Their eyes met and they shared a low, contented laugh.

"It's a good thing I left my suitcase here when I showered and changed last night." Grant's lips moved against hers as he spoke. "Otherwise, you'd be stuck here with no phone and a man with no clothes."

"That's right," Kelli murmured. "I forgot about the phone. But believe me, I wouldn't have minded about the clothes."

"It's also a good thing that I brought extra food with me. Because I just realized I'm starving."

"You can't be starving. It's too early to be starving."

"I am. What do you say we get up, go downstairs, and whip up something?"

"You'd leave this nice, warm bed and brave sub-zero temperatures to forage for food?"

"Well—" Grant's hand moved beneath her sweater "—I could probably be persuaded to do otherwise."

With a sultry smile she rolled on top of him, moved her hands along his body, and brought her lips to his in a leisurely kiss.

"Still want to get up?" she whispered, gently rocking her feminine core against that part of him which was already hard beneath her.

Bright desire glowed in eyes that had never seemed so blue. "I'm as up," he said breathlessly, "as I'll ever get."

WHEN THEY WOKE AGAIN LATER that morning, the storm was still raging—a heavy, powdery snowfall driven by freezing-cold winds.

"You are about to learn how to make perfect scrambled eggs." Dressed in his warmest clothes, Grant stood at the kitchen counter, whipping eggs and milk together in a bowl. "Here, you grate the cheese."

"When I put cheese in scrambled eggs, it sticks to the pan."

"It doesn't if you do it right."

Kelli dutifully grated the cheese, watching as he coated the pan with melted butter, then poured in the egg mixture when the butter was bubbling hot. When a fine layer of egg was cooked at the bottom, he added a few spices and stirred. At the last minute he added the cheese.

"Voila." He served the eggs onto plates heaped with fresh fruit and toast. "Eggs: fluffy. Cheese: melted. Pan: clean."

Kelli applauded, then bowed before him with admiration. "*Wunderbar, Herr Pembroke. Merveilleux, monsieur.* Sorry, I don't know how to say it in Italian. It is, without a doubt, the ideal Alpine breakfast. We'll call it *Oeufs a l'Alpine,* and suggest they include it on the menu at the Swiss Chalet."

Laughing, he grabbed her with one arm and pulled her to him. "You are my ideal Alpine breakfast." He kissed her softly. "And I don't know what it is, but I seem to have developed an insatiable appetite."

They may be snowed in, they decided later, but there was no reason why they couldn't work. They spent the afternoon in the studio, finishing the last of the comps for the collateral materials and going over the basics of what they needed for the media campaign.

With the bundle of wood Grant had brought in earlier they built a fire in the living-room hearth and relaxed that evening, wrapped in blankets, sipping hot chocolate.

"The simple life has its merits," Kelli admitted, as they ate delicious, foil-wrapped fish and potatoes they'd baked on charred embers at the side of the fire.

Afterward, Grant filled the oversize bathtub with hot water, and they eased into its soothing depths.

"I've always had this fantasy," Kelli told him, "of sharing a romantic, candlelit bubble bath with my lover while sipping champagne."

"Wait here just a minute." Grant left the bath, wrapped himself in a towel, and returned a few minutes later with several candles, a bottle of champagne, and two stemmed glasses.

"No bubble bath," he apologized, propping the lit candles in makeshift foil holders on the tile ledge above them, "but you've got candlelight, champagne, and your lover. Will three out of four do?"

Kelli laughed with delight. "Thank you. It's perfect. Absolutely perfect."

He opened the bottle of champagne, poured two glasses, and handed her one. Turning off the overhead lights, he slid back into the tub. The candles' combined flames cast a soft glow on their faces which faded into darkness around them. They touched their glasses gently together, then sipped the bubbly, sparkling wine.

Eyes locked with hers, Grant said in a dramatic, lowered tone: "Come quickly, I am tasting stars."

Kelli smiled, puzzled. "What?"

"That's what Dom Perignon famously exclaimed to his companions after his first taste of champagne."

"I love that. It's just right—the ideal description of this champagne."

"And it brings to mind yet another way," he said gruffly, setting both of their glasses aside, "to come quickly ... and taste stars." Eyes gleaming, he pulled her naked, willing, slippery body close to his.

~

"WHAT DO you say we forget the ad campaign?" Grant murmured.

The storm continued its blustery blow the following morning, covering the landscape in a veil of white. They'd moved their makeshift bed in front of the master bedroom's fireplace and had slept in front of its cozy warmth.

Grant sat on the floor behind Kelli, his long legs stretched out on either side of her, his arms wrapped around her waist, as they both stared into the mesmerizing flames. "Let's spend the rest of the week camped out here in front of the fire."

Kelli laughed. "You'd never forgive yourself if we did that."

"You're probably right. It's tempting, though. I never realized it could be so much fun to be snowed in."

"It *has* been fun." Kelli leaned her head back against his shoulder and sighed. "But we'd better get going. The storm could stop any time, and we still have to meet our deadline. If we put our heads together ...."

"Put our heads together? That sounds promising." He cupped her chin gently and tilted her mouth up to his. His kiss was slow and sweet, and she felt the stirrings of renewed desire, the desire that never seemed to diminish no matter how many times they made love.

I've never wanted anyone this way before, she thought. She wanted to let go of time and reason, to melt back against him. But then she remembered the reason they were there in the first place. She broke the kiss and took a deep breath.

"Grant, if we keep this up, we'll never get any work done."

"That depends on what you mean by *work*."

"This is *your* campaign. The account you were so hot to trot for a week ago. Remember?"

"I remember." He sighed, adjusting her within his arms until she was resting comfortably against his chest. "Okay. Let's try word association again."

She nodded and closed her eyes, remembering that they needed a series of ads that emphasized gambling, and a series with an Alpine theme—at least five or six different headlines in all. "I'll give you a word. You say the first thing that comes to mind. Ready?"

"Ready."

"Casino."

"Gamble."

"Gamble," she repeated.

"Frolic."

She tilted her head back and looked at him. "Gamble, frolic?"

"Gambol." He spelled it out loud.

She swatted his thigh playfully. A thought occurred to her and she said facetiously: "I've got it. We aren't allowed to say *gamble*—so we show a couple cavorting in the snow, and the same couple having fun at the craps table. *Gambol at Cassera's Tahoe.*"

He groaned.

"I knew you'd like it. You have such good taste."

"And you taste so good." His arms tightened around her and she felt his lips against her neck.

"Let's get serious now."

"Serious. Right. Go."

"Jackpot," she said.

"Win."

"Money."

"Pay."

"Game."

"Play."

"Pay, play ...." Kelli mused. "I know! How about: *It pays to play ... at Cassera's.*"

"Good."

She brightened. "You really think so?"

"I do. Harry's Club might frown if we used it, though. It's been their slogan for the past ten years."

"Oh." Kelli laughed. "No wonder it sounded so familiar." She closed her eyes again, leaned back against him. "Okay, let's start over. Blackjack."

"Deal."

"Cards."

"Hand."

"Poker."

"Bet."

"Chips."

"Eat."

"Stay on subject. Excitement."

"Sex."

"You're not concentrating!"

"I *am* concentrating." His hands slid up to cover her breasts. "Believe me, I'm concentrating."

The wonderful things his lips were doing to the side of her neck sent tingling sensations racing across the surface of her skin. "R—roulette."

"Wheel."

"Spin."

"Win." He laughed softly, his breath warming her cheek. "I've got it. We show a naked couple in one of the hotel rooms, a roulette wheel, and a roll of money. *Cassera's Tahoe. Sin. Spin. Win.*"

She couldn't help but join in his laughter. "Ted will love it. Guaranteed."

"He has good taste, too." Grant turned her until she was facing him, his lips moving tenderly across her face.

"Grant," she whispered. "Stop. I can't think …."

"Neither can I," he murmured. "So, let's stop trying." He kissed her mouth—a long, deep kiss—and this time she couldn't fight the desire that rose to meet his.

She wrapped her arms around his neck, forgetting everything but Grant and the moment and the joy and wonder of being in his arms.

THE NEXT MORNING, although the wind had died down, snow still fell steadily. With the deadline for the presentation looming nearer, they decided they'd better get down to some serious work.

They spent long hours tossing ideas back and forth, trying to come up with the catchy angles they needed for the campaign.

"We're going to wrap this thing right now." Grant paced slowly across the studio floor. "Clear your mind. Think: *Alpine*. Tell me the first thing you see."

"Julie Andrews."

"Julie Andrews??"

"In her nun's habit, standing in an Alpine meadow filled with wildflowers. Singing her heart out to the sky."

"That's great. Just great." Grant raised his eyes and hands to the ceiling as if asking for divine assistance. "We build an advertising campaign for a gambling establishment around a singing nun."

"You *said* to say the first thing that came to mind."

"I think we'd better try another approach."

They tried another approach, and then another, for several more hours. Nothing sparked an idea worth pursuing.

"This is ridiculous." Grant tossed his pencil onto the table in frustration. "We're not getting anywhere."

Kelli sat down at her drafting table and leaned her chin on her hand dejectedly. "We could use a few of those brilliant copywriters of yours about now."

"You're right." He went to the window and looked out. Snow was piled up in huge drifts around the house. "But even if the weather report's right, and the storm ends tomorrow, it'll be another day or two at least before they clear the roads. No one can get in, and we can't get out."

He sighed. "If I could just get a few of my people on the line, I'd drag them off their other projects for a few hours, have them start hashing out some ideas for us. But without a phone—"

Kelli felt guilty suddenly, knowing it was because of her that he was stuck here, cut off from the world, unable to keep tabs on the work at his office. Unable even to make any decent progress on their own work. "I'm sorry this is going so slowly."

"It's not your fault."

"When I work by myself, I usually come up with a list of ideas in just a few hours."

"So do I."

"Then why are we coming up empty-handed? It was such a breeze, doing the logo and the other comps, but when it comes to the ads ... You thought we'd make such a great team, and it hasn't worked out that way at all."

"We do make a great team," he said softly.

Her blood stirred as she met his gaze, recognizing that I-want-you look in his eyes. "I didn't mean *that* kind of team," she responded. Although in truth she'd been thinking about him precisely that way since the night they first met.

Grant came up behind her and wrapped his arms around her waist. "I think you were right about us. About what might happen if we got too involved. We got all that work done in the first few days because we were just business associates. We were attracted to each other, but we'd hardly touched. We hadn't made love. But now—if we had a chaperone to keep us apart, we'd probably have come up with seventeen brilliant ideas by now."

"Are you sorry, then, that we got involved?" she whispered.

He scooped one arm beneath her legs and lifted her off the stool. "Not for a second," he replied emphatically. And then his mouth found hers.

~

"It's like a fairyland!" Kelli cried the next morning, looking outside the window.

She could hardly wait to go outside. The landscape was covered with a soft, deep blanket of sparkling white. The sun shone in a blue sky and snow frosted the pine branches like whipped cream.

Her exhilaration in the beauty of the landscape faded when she saw the worried expression on Grant's face. He stared at the immense, curving mound of fresh snow beside the garage that had once been her car, and the long, winding driveway leading up to the road, now buried beneath four feet of new snow.

His van was parked at the far end of the drive, but even if they hiked to it and dug it out, it couldn't go anywhere until the road crew cleared the roads.

"Only three days left after today," Grant mused, frustrated, "and we've drawn a big fat zero on this campaign. We've got to try—somehow—to get out of here."

Only three more days.

Kelli nodded, realizing with a sudden pang of regret that their special time alone together was about to end. It had been a wonderful few days, the best of her life. But when the presentation was finished—*if* they ever finished it—would that be it for them?

They had never discussed the future. Grant had never

hinted that he wanted or expected anything more than this brief affair. And she'd made it clear that she wanted to live life solo, on her own terms, for the foreseeable future.

That *was* what she wanted ... right? Uncertain, she heaved a deep sigh and turned from the window.

They agreed to trek up to the other two houses within walking distance to see if anyone had a phone that worked. After dressing warmly, they plowed through the deep snow in their after-ski boots—an exhausting effort.

When they reached the second house, they were red-faced and out of breath. They found it deserted and locked up just as tight as the first.

"So much for that." Grant shrugged in resignation. "At least the road crew works quickly in this area. They ought to be up here by tomorrow."

When the road was clear, he explained, he'd get his van out, stop by a garage, and have them send a plow to clear the driveway down to the house. Meanwhile, there was nothing else they could do. They might as well sit tight and wait.

Grant's idea of sitting tight and waiting, however, had nothing to do with sitting.

"As long as we're out here," he said when they reached her Rover, "let's do something useful. Let's clear the snow off this thing."

"Shouldn't we go back in and get to work?" Kelli asked in surprise. They'd put in a few more hours in the studio the evening before, and to their disappointment, had gotten nowhere. "We're so short on time."

"I know. But if our creativity's dried up, it's because

we've been cooped up inside too long. A few hours off will do us both good."

With the shovel he'd brought, they dug out her car. Next, Grant suggested they install the new part he'd brought for her engine.

"Need any help?" he asked.

She cast him a sidelong glance. "Trust me, I've got this."

He stood at her side like a surgeon's assistant, watching her with a sharp eye as he handed her tools. "Wow," he said when she was done. "You did that like a pro."

"It was no big deal. Someday, if you want, I'd be happy to teach you a thing or two about cars."

He opened his mouth to say something, then apparently changed his mind. "Wouldn't that be nice." He seemed to be smothering a grin.

"You Mercedes owners are all alike. Stuck up." She grabbed a handful of snow and threw it at him, narrowly missing him when he ducked down behind the car. A second later a snowball came flying over the hood, splattering against her arm.

"Hey!" Kelli ducked down. "This means war!"

They exchanged snowballs, laughing and shouting, until their hats lay yards away and both their jackets and hair were laced with the powdery snow.

"Uncle!" Grant called, beckoning her to follow him up to the hillside above the house. "I have this urge to do something totally frivolous. Let's build a snowman."

Kelli was all for it. She hadn't built a snowman in years.

Grant, it seemed, was a champion snowman builder.

They created a big, round fellow on the hillside in front of the house, using tiny pinecones for eyes and nose and a small, curved stick for his smile. Grant added his ski hat and gloves, and when Kelli pointed out that it was chauvinistic to just build men out of snow, he agreed and they built a snow woman, complete with hourglass figure and a spray of long green pine needles for hair.

Grant retrieved Kelli's ski hat and adjusted it just so on the snow woman's head. "This couple is missing something."

Kelli pursed her lips, studying their handiwork as she might study a painting. "You're right." She turned to Grant and their gazes touched. "They look—" she began, and in unison they finished "—lonely."

Without another word, Grant knelt down and began forming a smaller heap of snow at the snow woman's side. Kelli joined in, laughing. Her fingers were starting to feel numb inside her gloves when, sometime later, two snow children with matching pine-needle hair smiled back at them from the hillside. At the snow people's feet reclined a snow dog with a lopsided muzzle and long floppy ears.

"Now *that's* what I call one happy family," Grant remarked.

By now the snow had begun to melt on the pines, and icicles danced from the branches like sparkling lights on a Christmas tree. Kelli breathed deeply of the cold, fresh air, letting go a sigh of the purest pleasure and contentment she'd ever known.

She felt lucky to be alive, lucky to be here, lucky to be sharing this beautiful day with Grant. She didn't want it ever to end.

"Gotcha!"

The shout came from behind. Suddenly she was down

in the soft snow, rolled onto her back with Grant on top of her. Her shriek was cut off abruptly by his possessive kiss. "Kelli," he said huskily, "you and I ...." He hesitated, and his lips tightened in a regretful frown. "You and I ought to get back to work."

She wondered what he'd been about to say. She ought to feel cold, lying on her back in Grant's arms, surrounded by powdery snow, but she didn't. Even through the layers of their heavy clothing, the heat of his body seemed to warm hers.

"We'll go in and make a fire," he added. "We'll talk this thing through. Sooner or later the ideas have to start flowing again."

"Right."

"In fact, I have an idea. It's not worked out yet, but I keep seeing it in the back of my mind. There's ...." He paused, brushed his lips against her temple. "Did I ever tell you that you have beautiful eyes?"

"Yes," she whispered, smiling now.

"And a beautiful nose?"

"Yes."

"And a beautiful mouth?" Their eyes met for a long, silent moment, and she knew hers shone with the same open affection she saw in his. He kissed her softly. "Now what was it that I was saying?"

"Something about an idea you had."

"No, before that."

"You were telling me how much work we're going to get done when we get back inside."

"Ah, yes. Why is it, when we're together, I always lose my train of thought?"

"Because," Kelli said with an impish grin, "you've developed a one-track mind."

"You're right. And the train's been on that same track since the night we met."

~

KELLI OPENED HER EYES. In the dim light, she noticed the empty space and untouched pillow beside her and heaved a deep sigh. Grant still hadn't come to bed.

She'd stayed up with him until well after midnight, reading and rereading their research books and the casino's existing brochures, going over their stacks of rejected ideas and sketches, and looking once more through Kelli's comps for the collateral materials.

They'd each come up with a few passable ideas for ads and had sketched them out. Nothing too bad, but nothing to get excited about, either. Finally, exhausted, she'd told him she had to go to bed.

"You go ahead," he'd said. "I'm going to keep at it for a while."

Kelli sat up now and looked across the studio. Grant sat at the table next to a single lamp, his head bent, his forehead furrowed in concentration. He held a pen poised over a notepad scribbled with writing. His hair was tousled, his cheeks were darkened by a day's growth of beard, and even from across the room she could see his eyes were bloodshot with weariness.

She felt the same dynamic pull she always felt when she looked at him. Yet a dart of anguish pierced her at the frustration she saw in his face.

"I'm sorry if I woke you," he said, not looking up.

"You didn't. Why are you still up? You must be exhausted."

"I'm fine."

"The work will still be there in the morning."

"It *is* morning," he said tightly.

She wrapped herself in a blanket and crossed to him. "It's three-thirty, Grant. You have to get some sleep."

"I couldn't sleep. Not now."

"Could we ask Ted for an extension? Because we were snowed in?"

"No way. He's heard rumors, remember? That my agency's slow, that we don't meet our deadlines? How will it look if we don't bring this in on time?"

"Not good." Sighing, she began to massage the muscles that pulled his neck and shoulders taut.

To her dismay, he tensed beneath her hands and said, "Don't."

She jerked back as if she'd just touched a hot brand. "Sorry. I just wanted to—"

"Don't apologize," he said abruptly. "Just go back to bed. It's my problem. There's no reason why we should both lose sleep over this."

"Since when did it become *your* problem?" She was both hurt and irritated. "We made a deal. We're in this together."

"Together we've come up with a big fat zero."

She'd said the same thing the day before, but now, he said the words with such disgust that they stung.

"Fine. I'll work here, and you work there. We'll see how we do on our own."

He didn't reply. Rubbing sleep from her eyes, she

grabbed a pencil and paper, turned on the lamp over her drafting table, and climbed up onto her stool. For the next hour, she tried to follow her usual procedure for coming up with a slogan: list key words and features of the product or place. Hit on the key benefit to the target audience. Try for a pun, an alliteration, or a clever turn of phrase.

But the silent tension in the room was deafening, and she couldn't think.

Outside, the wind rustled in the trees and water lapped against the shore. The sounds reminded her of the day they'd gone out in the boat on the lake.

The lake. She closed her eyes, remembering the vast, peaceful blueness that had stretched out toward the distant mountains. Recalling the beauty of the trees and the puffy clouds in a brilliant, sapphire sky.

That's it, she thought. *It was in front of our noses all the time.*

"Grant." Her voice seemed to echo in the enforced stillness of the room. He looked up at her. "I think we've been forgetting something. In all the hours we've been going over this, we've talked about gambling and skiing and mountains and God knows what else, but we haven't once talked about Tahoe's biggest draw."

He looked at her. "You mean the lake?" When she nodded, he added, "I was just thinking about that."

Funny, that they should both realize it at the same time. "Most of the ads run in this area, and the lake is the most identifiable landmark."

"*And* the primary reason a lot of people come here—not just to gamble." Grant chewed on the end of his pencil. "If we could use the lake as a primary focus, come up with a theme that ties it in with Cassera's—"

"Isn't Cassera's the biggest high rise in Stateline?" she asked.

"Yes."

"Which makes it another identifiable landmark?"

"Yes. To the people who know Tahoe."

"Okay, so why don't we take a sensational photograph that highlights both?"

He leaned forward in his chair, making a frame with his hands. "Pine trees in the foreground. In the center, distant, we see Cassera's poking out above the trees."

"Behind it, the lake stretching out in all its glory. Beyond, snow-covered mountains and lots of sky."

He stood up and rubbed his chin thoughtfully as he paced the room. "I can see it. It's just the look I wanted. We put in Cassera's new logo where you can't miss it, and a big bold headline—" He stopped, palms up, searching. "We need a slogan that contrasts with the beauty of the scene. Back to the gambling idea. Give me some gambling slang and see if one fits."

"Go for broke."

"Double or nothing."

Ideas flew back and forth.

Grant kept shaking his head. "It's got to fit with the lake, or mountains, or sky. Let me think." He strode the length of the room and back, muttering to himself. Pacing back and forth. Like a caged tiger, she thought.

"What if—" He went back to his table and wrote something, still standing, then crossed it out. Kelli scribbled out a few ideas of her own. Nothing was quite right.

"Damnit!" Grant crumpled up the sheet he'd been writing on and threw it into the trash. "Where the hell are those snowplows? How much longer are we going to be stuck here? This is such a waste of time."

Tired and irritable, Kelli leaned both elbows on her drafting table and massaged her temple. "I hate wasting time too, Grant. I haven't had any workmen here in almost a week. The house is way behind schedule. It'll never be finished on time."

"The house isn't the only thing that won't be finished on time," he snapped. "Two days to go and we haven't even come up with one decent idea."

She let out a long breath. "I'm sorry things haven't worked out the way you'd planned. But if you recall, this setup wasn't my idea. You proposed it."

"Don't you think I know that?" He whirled on her. "I took a gamble, coming up here. Put all my eggs in one basket. But I figured if things didn't go well, I could call an emergency creative session with my staff and pull the thing off. What I didn't count on was the storm, being snowed in here while the clock kept ticking. I didn't count on wasting five days in a creative washout. And I didn't count on—"

His eyes darted to meet hers, and then he flung himself away again. "I should have known better than to come back here after I left. I should have called things off long before the storm, put my people on double overtime. We would have finished this whole thing a week ago."

Called things off before the storm? Kelli thought in dismay. Canceled out all those wondrous, loving days they'd shared? Didn't she mean a thing to him?

Obviously not. The campaign was the only thing that mattered.

Hurt and despair rose in her chest and she burst out, "Fine! Cancel them out if you want. Pretend they never happened. I'm sorry if I didn't perform to your expectations, but I'm sure if you just hike up to the highway and catch a ride to San Francisco, that hotshot staff of yours will come up with seventeen smashing slogans in no time. When it comes to talent, I can see *they've* got the corner on the market. The sky's the limit. So why don't you go get a flashlight and—"

"Wait, what? Hold on. What did you say?"

"I said go get a flashlight." When had she started to cry? Kelli moved to the door, wiping tears from her cheeks. "There's one in the kitchen. You're in a hurry, aren't you? No time to lose. The clock keeps ticking. So, get out of here, before—"

"Stop, would you?" He crossed the room and grabbed her by the shoulders.

"You just said it, Kelli. The perfect slogan. Exactly what we've been looking for!"

CHAPTER 9

It took Kelli a moment, her mind working backward over what she'd just said, and then she understood.

The Sky's the Limit.

An image formed in her mind: the bold headline set in a huge field of sky above Cassera's casino. Above the lake.

It was catchy. It was memorable. It had visual impact. It would work. "I like it."

"So do I."

They both started talking at once, jotting down the gist of the balance of the copy, outlining a few other ads that would have a different look but use the same slogan.

Kelli forgot their prior argument, felt an adrenaline surge, and saw the rising excitement in his eyes as new ideas came to their minds simultaneously. Gesticulating with enthusiasm, they interrupted each other, sentence fragments darting back and forth, thoughts started by one and finished by the other.

They came up with a whole series of ads to go with the

first one, centered on a skiing theme—snow skiing for winter, waterskiing for summer.

A shot of Cassera's with the snow-covered slopes of Heavenly Valley behind it: *Cassera's Tahoe: Skiing Is Believing.*

A collage of photos of the mountains and lake with a snow skier and a water-skier: *See. Ski.*

To highlight Cassera's restaurants—a place to relax after a day on the slopes—a young couple in love, sitting at a table in the cafe, light sparkling on stemmed glasses of champagne, forks crossed as they share steaming bites of cheese fondue: *Apres-ski.*

Their success seemed to open a dam of pent-up creativity, and all at once a flood of new, even more exciting ideas came spilling out—so fast they could hardly keep up with them.

The second theme they'd been struggling with all week fell into place. The campaign focused on gambling. Each ad highlighted a different game or group of games in the casino, and the headlines they came up with didn't just click, they sang.

A close-up of a winning blackjack hand: *Feel Twenty-one Again.*

A view of the casino's dance floor spliced in with a hand shooting craps: *Rock 'N' Roll.*

A slot machine hitting a jackpot, pouring out so much money it had burst into flame: *Hot Slots.*

A roulette wheel combined with a baccarat dealer in action: *Wheel and Deal.*

At the end of a few heated hours and two pots of coffee, they had a stack of rough thumbnail sketches. Kelli felt punch-drunk. She sank into the chair by the window and closed her eyes.

"What time is it? What day is it? Do we have enough ideas yet? Can we quit now?"

"Yes, we can quit." Grant's voice was infused with exhaustion, yet it held a jubilant note that made her heart feel as light as her head. She heard him collapse into the other chair. "And in answer to the rest of your questions, it's 6:30 A.M., it's Wednesday, and we have enough ideas now to last three seasons. Maybe a couple of years."

"Good. Because my mind just filed a complaint. It shut down for the winter. Went into hibernation. Kaput. History."

He chuckled softly. "I knew we'd make a good team from the moment I met you. I *knew* it."

She was about to agree, when their argument slipped back into her mind. *I didn't count on wasting five days in a creative washout. I should have called things off long before the storm.* The hurt and anger she'd felt came back in a rush and she took a long, deep breath, waiting for it to subside.

"I guess we do make a good team, Grant," she said quietly. "But only when we're both hot, steaming mad."

There was a moment of silence, and then she heard him get up from his chair and cross to her side. She felt his hand on her arm and she opened her eyes.

"I'm sorry about what happened before." He knelt beside her. She could see how tired he was. Yet hope and regret mingled in his direct gaze. "I'm sorry for the things I said. I didn't mean any of it. I'm exhausted, I haven't slept. I was so frustrated."

He lifted her hand to his lips and kissed it. "You're a

very talented woman, Kelli. I should have been thanking you for everything you've done on this project, not ranting and raving about what wasn't finished. But I want you to know ... what I feel for you is a lot more than gratitude."

The warmth in his eyes, the touch of his lips and hand, worked their way into her heart. "Is it?" she asked, all at once breathless with hope. Would he tell her he loved her? Could she reveal, now, how she felt about him?

"Yes. Coming up here, leaving the company for days at a time so I could work with you—it's so out of character for me I could hardly believe I was doing it. At first, I told myself it was just business. You have extraordinary talent, and I wanted you on this job. That was true, but it wasn't the only reason I came up here. It took me a while to admit it to myself, but ...."

He stood, pulling her into his embrace. "Once I'd met you, I couldn't get you out of my mind. You'd refused the job I offered. You were only going to be here for a few weeks. I had to do something, and fast. I know I was unforgivably pushy. I backed you into a corner to get you to work with me. But I had to do it. I couldn't take the chance you'd say no."

"I'm glad you did it," she admitted. "I wouldn't trade these past weeks for anything."

"Neither would I." He cradled her head against his shoulder and held her for a long, silent moment. "You're a very special lady, Kelli, and you mean a lot to me."

You mean a lot to me. She squeezed her eyes shut, her heart heavy, knowing now that she could never tell him she loved him.

Maybe it's better this way, she decided, wishing she

didn't suddenly feel like crying. When we're finished here, when we say goodbye, there won't be any binding ties. No promises to break. He can go his way, and I can go mine.

"I wish," he went on, his head drooping with fatigue, "I could take you downstairs and make love to you right now. But I'm so tired, the minute you put me in a horizontal position I'll fall asleep."

She took a deep breath, steeling herself. "Why don't you go catch a few hours, then? I'll start working on these comps."

"I don't have time for sleep. I have to write additional copy for some of the ads. And you'll need help on these comps if we're going to finish by Friday morning."

"I don't need help. We've got two days, Grant. If I start now, I can have them finished in time."

He looked at her in surprise, then chuckled softly. "That's right. I forgot that I'm working with Seattle's Quick Draw Champion, two years running."

"Three." She batted him on the arm. "And don't make fun of me. Now go lie down and sleep before you collapse."

"Aren't you tired, too? You said your brain was on the fritz. You only got a few hours' sleep."

"I'm fine. To tell you the truth, I'm itching to get started."

"Okay." He moved across the room toward their sleeping area, adding: "But if you hear anything that sounds like a snowplow, please wake me up. I've been out of touch with my office far too long. I need to get to a telephone today, even if we have to hike out of here."

Kelli sat down to work with renewed energy, breezed

through a pencil comp for one of the ads, and started on another.

The early-morning sun filled the room with golden light when, a few hours later, she heard the shower running and Grant's cheerful whistling. She'd been so engrossed in her work she hadn't even noticed him get up. After a while he appeared from the bathroom, freshly shaven, dressed in jeans and a sweater.

"How's it going?"

She gestured for him to take a look at the *Apres-ski* ad she was sketching. He came up behind her, rested both hands on the edge of the drafting table and leaned his cheek against hers. "I like."

He smelled wonderful, of shampoo and soap and the cologne that she loved. "I'm glad," she said as he began kissing her neck. "I wasn't sure if you'd want such a close-up of the two people, but I thought it was a little sexier, with—"

"I wasn't," he whispered, "talking about the ad."

"Oh."

"What you've drawn is very good." His hands left the table to capture her breasts. "But what I really like is *you*. The way you feel. I missed you. It's no fun sleeping alone, with you halfway across the room. I think—" He stopped, listening.

A sound caught at the edge of her awareness. A distant roaring, like the whirr of the electric saws. No, no like the sound of heavy machinery.

The sound of ....

Their eyes met at the same moment. "Snowplows!"

By the time they reached the road, the plow had passed

by, heaping a ton of snow on top of Grant's van at the roadside.

"Come on," Grant said much, much later, when they'd finally cleared the van and cleaned the windshield. "We have to get to a phone."

They climbed into the van and headed south to Stateline, where they stopped at the first gas station they came to.

"You might want to give your brother a call." Grant parked in front of the phone booth. "And try to get ahold of the phone company to fix your line. I'll see if I can get this guy to clear your driveway."

Kelli called the phone company first. They assured her that if they couldn't fix the problem from their office, they'd send someone out on Friday. So many phones out of order, they couldn't possibly get there sooner.

Next, she placed the call to her brother's office. She was put through immediately.

"Kelli!" Kyle sounded relieved. "Where are you? Are you all right?"

"I'm fine. I thought you might be worried, so—"

"I've been frantic. They said the airport and roads were closed, and I couldn't get through to you. I hoped you'd gotten out before the storm. I called Grant's office Monday, and they told me he was up at Tahoe. Is he with you?"

"Yes. We didn't realize it was going to be such a blizzard until it was too late. We've been snowed in at the house."

"All this time?"

"Yeah. They just cleared the road a few minutes ago."

"I'm so sorry. If I'd thought ...."

"Don't be sorry. We ended up making good use of the time," she replied, a teasing note in her voice.

There was a pause, and then he laughed. "Well, what do you know. My little sister Kelli. I never would have guessed."

She noticed Grant waiting anxiously to use the phone. "I have to go, Kyle. Grant needs to call his office. Everything's been going fine on the house. Now that the storm's over I can make up for lost time. I'll call you in a few days and give you a more detailed update." They said goodbye and she hung up. "Next."

"Thanks." While Grant placed a call, he told her, "The guy's going to follow us back and clear your driveway. He gave me some line about being too busy, but I offered to double his rate so he—" Grant turned back to the phone. "Hi, Charlene."

Kelli lifted her face to the warm sunshine. Such a treat after so many days of freezing cold. Traffic whizzed by on the highway and the gas station was crowded, but the pines were laden with snow and she heard Christmas music from someone's car radio drifting on the breeze. She'd almost forgotten that Christmas was coming, less than two weeks away.

She'd have the comps done by tomorrow. The presentation was due the next day. If she scheduled workmen like crazy, she might be able to have the floors and carpet laid and furniture delivered before Kyle and his family got here.

Everything was going to be all right.

"Carl! How goes it?" she heard Grant say. And then: "Heard what?"

His sudden change of tone made Kelli turn. His shoulders were tense, his forehead lined with anxiety.

"Which account?" he asked curtly. There was a pause, and then he cursed under his breath. "That should have been finished three days ago. Where's Andy?" Grant's mouth opened in surprise. "What do you mean, he left? Where did he go?" Practically spitting out the word, he said, "Dawson!"

Kelli froze in alarm. She remembered Grant mentioning Andy, his creative director. While he was gone, Grant had given Andy complete control of creative, under Carl, the executive vice-president. Andy was a talented guy, Grant had said. The best. He'd been with him for five years.

And now he'd quit? To work for Bob Dawson?

"So. Bob's been up to his old tricks again. Terrific. Any more good news or is that it?" Grant listened for a long moment. At first his face registered surprise, then frustration, then barely repressed anger.

"After all I went through to land that account ... this is ridiculous. Another few days wouldn't kill them, if Dawson wasn't shooting off his mouth. See if you can stall them. We'll get the thing to them tomorrow ... I don't know how, Carl. I'll figure something out. How many are there? ... Nothing's impossible. Tell Jim to find another illustrator ... Okay, okay. Set up a meeting, then, for this afternoon. I'll placate them somehow."

Grant checked his watch. It was just past nine. "It'll take me three hours to get there, maybe more," he went on, "and I'll need time to change, go over a few things. Make it as late as possible. Four-thirty." Hanging up, he cursed again.

Signaling for the snowplow driver to follow, he headed straight for the van, frowning furiously.

Kelli hurried after him and got in. He gunned the engine. Her heart thumped in alarm as she waited for him to explain. Finally, when they were halfway back to the house, he heaved a deep sigh and looked at her, his hands gripping the wheel.

"One of our brand-new accounts, The Harrington Company, is threatening to pull out if we don't deliver a job *today*. They're real-estate developers. We're doing a brochure for them. Everything was going fine. Now Bob Dawson's spreading his rumors, saying we're slow as molasses and don't meet our deadlines. Only this time he got smart and made sure it came true." Grant let out a short, sarcastic laugh.

"Andy was in charge of the Harrington job," he continued. "He obviously knew well in advance that he was leaving to work for Dawson, because he let it slide. My people put in an all- nighter, but Andy farmed out the illustrations and what came back this morning is pure garbage. My senior art director's out with the flu, Andy's gone—they're my only two illustrators. The client wants the whole job or nothing, and they want it by the end of the day or they're pulling out."

"Oh, Grant. I'm so sorry."

"It's not your fault," he snapped. "It's mine. It was my decision to come up here. You, as you so clearly pointed out this morning, tried to talk me out of it."

His words stung, and she fell silent. After a moment his features softened and he reached across, gave her leg a gentle squeeze.

"I'm sorry. I shouldn't be lashing out at you. It's Andy I'm mad at, and Dawson, and the entire Harrington Company. I was looking forward to finishing the Cassera's job with you, now that we're finally on course again, and now I have to go back to the city."

"Can I help? Can I come with you? I could do the illustrations you need, and—"

"No. You stay right here. Finish those comps. Let's at least get one job delivered on time. I'll have one of my writers do the copy and I'll be back here bright and early for the meeting Friday morning."

"But ... what if you don't like the way I do them? If you don't come back until Friday, there won't be time to make any changes before the meeting."

He gave her a reassuring smile. "I'll like them. I trust you. Besides, you can't leave. The house is behind schedule. Once this guy clears the driveway, you can get your carpet layers and hardwood floor installers to finish the place and make your brother one happy man."

His tone was lightly sarcastic, but she knew he didn't mean to be cutting. He had good reason to be in a foul mood, and in fact he was right. She *did* have to finish the job for Cassera's, and her place was here, finishing the house as she'd promised.

But the thought of Grant leaving under these circumstances made her feel miserable. No need to make an issue out of it, she decided. He felt bad enough already.

She swallowed hard. "I'll miss you."

"I'll miss you too, babe." He reached out to gently caress her shoulder as he drove. "The next few days aren't going to be any picnic."

~

KELLI TUCKED her pencil behind her ear and leaned forward on the drafting table, resting her head on her hands.

Barely an hour had passed since Grant had left. The snowplow had just finished clearing the driveway. The house was so silent she thought she'd go out of her mind.

When Grant had stood at the roadside and kissed her goodbye, it had taken all her strength not to throw herself into his van and go with him. But he'd insisted she could help him best by staying put and finishing the job for Cassera's.

Not knowing what else to do, she'd gone straight to her drafting table to finish the *Apres-ski* comp. But she couldn't get Grant and his problems out of her mind.

Despite his reassurances, she felt the mess was her fault, at least partly. She felt certain, if he'd been in San Francisco the past week where he belonged, his creative director wouldn't have flown the coop. Grant would have seen it coming and no doubt persuaded him to stay.

It was too late to get Andy back, but she couldn't bear the thought of Grant losing an account because of her as well.

She sat up, thinking.

Grant needed an illustrator. That was her specialty.

He was meeting the client today at four-thirty. She had Grant's business card, knew the address of his agency, and she had a map of the city. If she left now, she could probably be there by two o'clock.

If there weren't too many illustrations, and if they

weren't complicated, she might be able to finish them before the end of the day and he could deliver them. Grant had told her to stay put, but he couldn't refuse her help once she was there. He'd meet his deadline, and the client would be satisfied.

But what about the house? The driveway was clear. After a six-day hiatus she could finally make some calls, arrange to have workmen here tomorrow.

No, she decided. The house could wait. Grant's client couldn't.

She didn't hesitate. In fifteen minutes, she'd showered and dressed in the only businesslike outfit she had—the gray wool skirt and silk blouse she'd worn to the meeting with Ted at Cassera's. Throwing a few things into a suitcase, she gathered up the thumbnail sketches for the rest of the comps. She'd work her fingers off tomorrow, finish them at Grant's agency. She put everything in her car and left.

Her watch read one-thirty when the freeway signs began to read Berkeley, and she glimpsed the Bay Bridge. She took in an excited breath, forgetting her mission for the moment. She'd been here only a couple of weeks before for the interview with Bob Dawson, but then she'd been in a hurry to get to Tahoe and it had taken her so long to find her way through the city's confusing, congested streets, she'd had to leave without even a glimpse of the famous wharf.

Now, knowing she'd be able to stay for at least a day or two, she let herself be caught up in the spell of the bay and the city before her.

The bridge seemed to fly across the water, linking the

East Bay cities with the hills of San Francisco on the other side. A mass of skyscrapers clustered next to the shore. On either side, brightly colored rectangular houses clung to the slopes like stair steps.

The bay sparkled, dotted with boats and hovering sea gulls, even bigger than Lake Tahoe and with a different kind of beauty and excitement. As if it had a sense of its own importance, felt the pulse of a city alive and in love with itself.

The scene struck a chord in her memory. Suddenly she was eleven years old again, on holiday. Holding her father's hand. Watching the fishing boats at the wharf. Laughing with her brother and sisters as they tore into a loaf of sourdough bread. Smelling the fish and the salt in the air. It was seventeen years ago, yet she remembered as if it were yesterday.

Kelli felt an insane urge to forget the work, forget the problems Grant was facing, and spend the rest of the day sight-seeing. The idea made her laugh out loud. If everything went according to plan, she'd get Grant out of this jam this afternoon, finish the Cassera's job tomorrow, and have enough time left over for a night on the town.

She had just crossed the Bay Bridge when another thought struck her. What was Grant's staff going to think of her, barging in like this? Grant must have told them who he was working with at Tahoe. You didn't stay snowed in with a woman for days on end without raising a few eyebrows.

Wouldn't it be obvious to everyone exactly what the two of them had been up to? No way would that help her credibility. How could she expect anyone to respect her?

Don't worry, she told herself. Grant will smooth things over. Still, the temptation to turn back was so strong she had to grit her teeth and grip the wheel.

He needs you, Kelli. You're almost there. Go through with it.

It took her a while to find the place. Map in one hand, the steering wheel in the other, she fought through congestion on the busy streets, missed turns, passed one-way streets that always seemed to go the wrong way, and tried streets that ended in dead ends. Finally, she turned onto Union Street, and with a relieved sigh saw that she was in the right block.

Near the San Francisco marina, in an older section of town, the street was lined with restored buildings in a variety of architectural styles, housing little bakeries, delis, restaurants, clothing stores, and other small businesses. She liked the area at once. It had character.

She recognized Grant's agency from a vivid description he'd given her one evening. She smiled in delight. The Victorian house, three stories tall, was freshly painted in a rich cream color, with delicate gingerbread trim in a dark forest green—just as lovely as she'd pictured.

She found a small parking lot at the back but saw with alarm that the space marked *Pembroke* was empty. It was only two-fifteen. Where was Grant? She couldn't go ahead with her plan if he wasn't there to approve it. Could she?

Unsure what to do, Kelli walked around to the front and pushed open the heavy, oak door. Inside she stopped, taken aback for a moment by the beauty of the place.

The lobby was large, dominated by a wide oak staircase with a matching banister. It was furnished in dark oak and decorated in a French country theme—forest green and ivory, with burgundy accents. Plants in strategically placed wicker baskets gave the room a cozy feel, and the high bay windows filled the room with light.

A sofa, antique tables, and chairs were grouped in a cozy comer, and the walls were hung with row upon row of framed awards the agency had won.

It was warm and inviting, yet at the same time sophisticated and highly professional looking. Nothing like the offices of Thompson & McGuire, where she'd worked before—a cold, modem place of glass and steel. And a far cry from her own "office" at home—a drafting table set up in a corner of her living room.

"May I help you?"

Kelli started, remembering why she was here. A lovely, impeccably dressed woman rose to her feet behind the receptionist's desk. Her nameplate read Charlene Wong.

Hesitantly, Kelli went forward. Before she could say anything, a stocky man with a neatly trimmed red beard hurried down the stairs, carrying a huge cardboard folder that Kelli guessed held artwork.

"Char!" He handed the receptionist the folder. "Pace Printing is sending a messenger to pick this up in the next half hour. And I need to talk to Grant. Do you know where he is?"

Charlene smiled at Kelli, said she'd be with her in just a moment, and turned back to the man. Kelli stood to one side, listening with growing apprehension. Grant, it seemed, had just left to meet a client at a restaurant, and after that was heading straight for a meeting at The Harrington Company at four-thirty. Carl, the vice-president, was with him, along with someone named Marc, no doubt an account executive.

"Can you call and leave a message for him at the restaurant?" the bearded man asked.

Charlene shrugged helplessly. "Sorry, Jim. He didn't tell me where he was going. I could call the client and ask."

"Do that."

Charlene apologized again to Kelli for making her wait and made a quick call. She hung up, shaking her head. "They don't know which restaurant either."

"Now what?" Jim sighed. "No way to reach him until four-thirty. I don't know what to tell this guy."

"Who? What's wrong?" Charlene asked.

"It's the job for Harrington. The illustrator Grant asked for isn't available until Monday. I have to commit now or never for his price and Monday because he's got another offer. But Grant might not want to wait that long."

Kelli's heart began to hammer with nervous excitement. She was an illustrator. She was here, now, and she'd do the work for free. She'd hoped to have Grant give her the go-ahead, but he wasn't available—and time was running out. She was about to introduce herself when Jim swore and shook his head in disgust.

"If it wasn't for that stupid broad in Tahoe, we wouldn't be in this mess in the first place. Grant wouldn't have let Andy farm out those illustrations. If he'd been here instead of—"

Charlene's eyes slid to Kelli and back again. "Jim," she warned sternly.

He swore again. "Now I'm stuck trying to pick up the pieces."

Kelli took a step back, her cheeks burning. She'd been afraid these people wouldn't think much of her, but this was even worse. They were blaming her for what had happened. She understood why; she'd blamed herself.

But how could she introduce herself now? If Jim's indiscreet remarks mortified her, he'd feel even worse if he knew who she was.

Jim turned and looked at her for the first time. His frown disappeared. He held up a hand apologetically. "Sorry to leave you standing there like that. A few problems, nothing beyond our control. Charlene, take over." He backed away.

"No, wait, it's you I've come to see," Kelli said, making a quick decision. "You're Jim, the …." she paused, fishing.

"Production supervisor," he replied with a nod.

"Right." She smiled, trying to ignore the loud drum of her heart. "Grant Pembroke just told me you need an illustrator, pronto. So, I came right over. I'm ready to work."

His eyes brightened in surprise. "An hour ago, Grant was on my back to find someone. Where'd he run into you?"

"In … an elevator," she replied.

"Well, terrific! You just made my day. Come on up."

She followed him up the stairs thinking: *you did it, Kelli, and you didn't tell a single lie.*

"Grant wanted to deliver this today, but I told him there's no way. If you can finish by tomorrow, though—"

"How many illustrations do you need?"

"Four. Two spots and two full-page. It's for a new condo complex."

"Where is The Harrington Company? How long would it take to get there from here?"

"It's about a fifteen-minute drive."

Kelli checked her watch. That gave her a little less than two hours. "If I finish this by four-fifteen, can you find someone to deliver it to the meeting?"

Jim stopped at the doorway to the art department, a large sunny room where Kelli saw three artists bent over their drafting tables.

"Lady," he said, with a skeptical lift of his brows, "if you finish this by four-fifteen, I'll deliver it myself. Right after I eat my hat."

CHAPTER 10

Traffic crawled. Kelli drummed her fingers on the steering wheel, then checked her watch again.

Four-thirty-five. "How much farther?" she asked.

Jim, sitting beside her in her car, shrugged his wide shoulders. "Couple of miles. But at this rate, it might take half an hour."

"I could get there faster by walking."

"Not in those heels, you wouldn't."

Kelli remembered the high-heeled pumps she was wearing and sighed. Jim was right.

Inching forward through the San Francisco rush-hour traffic, they'd passed streets that soared up hills and seemed to disappear at the top. Even if she knew where she was going, which she didn't, the streets were too steep to move anywhere fast on foot.

"I still can't believe you finished those drawings. Never saw anyone work so fast." Jim ran his fingers through his thick, red hair and glanced aside at her with a grin. "Here I thought you'd tricked my brilliant, rational boss into an absurd working arrangement. And then you turn out to be a bona fide *artiste.* One of the best I've ever seen. And I've seen a lot of artists."

"Thank you." Kelli smiled to herself.

Jim hadn't thought to ask her name until she was halfway done with the last illustration. When she'd finally introduced herself and extended her hand he'd just stared at her, speechless, his face turning the same shade as his beard and hair.

Later, after she'd finished with ten minutes to spare, he'd apologized for his rude remarks in the lobby, and she'd admitted that Grant hadn't really sent her. She'd come on her own and hoped Grant wouldn't mind. Jim had laughed, then, and reassured her it was all right.

It did seem to be all right, except that she'd gotten stuck making the delivery. She'd hoped to stay in the background of all this, but most of Grant's employees took public transportation, and the few with cars were all up to their ears in work.

They would have made it to the meeting just before it started if traffic had moved. Now they were almost a half-hour late, and Kelli was getting nervous, wondering if this was such a good idea after all.

No doubt Grant was explaining to the client at this very moment why the art wouldn't be ready until Monday. Would it make him look like an idiot if she showed up with the art at the door?

At last, traffic opened up. In a few minutes they reached the building that housed The Harrington Company and left her car in a nearby parking structure. Once inside the office, Jim gave his name and asked the receptionist to call Grant out of the meeting. Kelli stood a distance behind him, waiting and worrying.

In what seemed less than a minute Grant appeared around a corner. It had been a while since she'd seen him in anything but casual clothes, and she felt a magnetic jolt at how attractive, masculine, and professional he looked in his three-piece suit. He didn't appear to see her at first, walked straight up to Jim with a questioning look on his face.

"Jim. What's up?"

"Got a little package here your client might be interested in," Jim replied. "It's finished. Thanks to your artist friend."

"My artist friend?" Grant, confused, took the oversize art briefcase from him.

Jim nodded, glancing over his shoulder at Kelli as he stepped aside.

Grant's eyes flashed to hers. Kelli's heart pounded as she watched a succession of emotions cross his face. Surprise. Dawning understanding. And a hint of an incredulous smile.

He removed one of the art boards from the briefcase. He lifted the cover sheet and studied it, his smile growing wider. In a few quick strides he was at her side, his eyes glowing.

"Looks like I've just spent half an hour buttering up somebody for nothing."

Her heart soared. She had to bite her lip to keep from grinning.

"Thank you," he said softly.

No response seemed adequate. She ached to touch him. But she couldn't, not here in this lobby in full view of Jim and the client's receptionist. So, she only smiled with her eyes, telling him *I did it for you.*

"Why don't you join us in the meeting?"

Kelli shook her head quickly, finding her voice. "No! No. I wouldn't have even come, but no one else had a car."

"I'm glad you came." He turned back to Jim and thanked him. "I know it's quitting time, but can you hang around a few minutes until the meeting's over?"

"Sure, boss."

Grant smiled at Kelli again and gestured toward a couch in the lobby. "Sit. I'll try to make this brief."

About twenty minutes later, Grant and his two colleagues reappeared, laughing and shaking hands with a group of very happy looking businessmen, who congratulated them on the excellent artwork and expressed how pleased they were to be working together.

Kelli felt a surge of excitement and relief that it had all worked out. She was even more thrilled when Grant introduced her to both his clients and his associates as the illustrator who'd come through for them.

Grant arranged for Carl to drive Jim and Marc back to the office in the company car. When she was back in her own parked car, with Grant behind the wheel—she'd decided he knew the area best, so she handed him the keys —he sat for a long moment, watching her, a heart-stirring combination of gratitude and affection on his face.

"Come here," he growled finally, as he pulled her across the front seat into his arms. "You've been known to pull some crazy stunts, but that was by far the craziest."

She wrapped her arms around his neck and looked up at him, eyes shining. "It was pretty impulsive, I know."

"Sometimes impulsive actions are best. If you think and worry too much, you can miss your only chance to act." He kissed her. "How on earth did you pull that off? Did you leave Tahoe five minutes after I did?"

"Sixty-five minutes. I had to wait for the guy to finish clearing the driveway."

"That's right."

She told him how she'd found his agency, even the details about her run-in with Jim.

"I'm sorry you had to hear all that. I thought a lot of Jim up until now, but—"

"Please, don't chastise him. He thinks the world of you, Grant. And we're friends now. I think I managed to win his respect."

"*That* doesn't surprise me. I wish I could have seen his face when you whipped up those illustrations in nothing flat." With a teasing smile he added, "I suppose you finished the whole batch of comps for Cassera's in the sixty-five minutes before you left? Or maybe you sketched with one hand while you were driving down here?"

"No." She laughed. "I thought I'd do them tomorrow at your office, if that's okay with you. Then we can follow each other back to Lake Tahoe Friday morning."

"A good plan." He smiled. "You know, it would have been a lot easier if I'd just let you come with me in the first place."

"It would have."

"What's next on the agenda? Dinner? At the wharf?"

"Sounds good to me."

He looked lovingly into her eyes. "Kelli," he said, his voice husky, "I'm glad you're here with me."

His arms tightened around her, and this time his kiss was long and deep. When their lips parted, they were both out of breath. "How about we forget dinner and go to my place?" He started the car's engine. "For once, I'd like to make love to you in a real, live *bed*."

THEY TUMBLED into Grant's big, brass bed the moment they reached his house, and made love slowly, luxuriously, a union so sweet and gentle and satisfying, Kelli felt her senses had been spoiled for anything else. Then they slept deeply, exhausted from the long, eventful day and the previous night without sleep.

Sometime in the middle of the night Kelli awakened to Grant's kisses on her neck as his arms drew her into his embrace.

"Speaking of kids," he whispered against her ear, "what do you think of them?"

The question brought her from sleep to groggy wakefulness with a small laugh. "I love kids." Kelli happily nestled within his arms.

"So do I. Did I ever tell you I used to babysit?"

She loved these late-night conversations that had been occurring in between slumber and lovemaking ever since they'd first slept together. They'd talked about everything, covering a wide range of subjects from childhood to the present, and everything she'd learned about him only whetted her appetite to learn more.

"When did you babysit?" she murmured sleepily.

"Ever since I can remember. I was the oldest, so I stood in for my parents a lot. When I was twelve, I started babysitting for a family down the street. Two girls and a boy." He sounded nostalgic. "I loved being with those kids. Talking to them, playing with them, reading to them. At times they'd say the most surprising and enlightening things."

Kelli rearranged herself so that she could glance at him across the pillows. The room was partially illuminated by moonlight through the blinds, and she was touched by the affection she saw in his face. She could just see him, some-day, getting down on the floor with his children, tinkering with their toys, helping with their homework, teaching them to appreciate Mozart and Monet and explaining about the rotation of the earth.

"You'll make a wonderful father someday."

"And you'll make a wonderful mother." He kissed her. "How many kids do you want?"

"Two."

"I'd like four. Two of each. I figured you would, too, coming from a big family."

"A big family was great fun for us kids—but it was so hard on my parents. They never had time for themselves. I can't remember them ever taking a vacation alone together until after I graduated from college." She rolled to her back and let out a sigh. "My oldest sister has this long-standing joke, saying my folks should have stopped after two kids. They always protest, insisting they couldn't give any of us up, but she's probably right."

Grant raised himself on one elbow, a twinkle in his

eyes. "I, for one, am glad your parents didn't stop after just two kids."

His arms wound around her and then he was kissing her shoulder, her throat, her cheek, until their mouths met, opening to each other. As his hands slowly, tenderly explored her body, she slid her hands along the warm hollows and hard, defined muscles of his shoulders, back, and buttocks.

"Beautiful," she whispered.

"You are." His voice was low and rough.

He kissed her breasts, his lips moving slowly against the softness of her skin. When they joined together, the sharing of the past weeks became the sharing of their bodies, gentle loving giving way to rising peaks of passion that brought them higher and higher until they stopped, hovering weightless on the edge of pure feeling, and then fell into blinding brightness, an echoing descent as brilliant and thunderous as an electrical storm.

Afterward they lay spent in each other's arms, legs entwined, gazing at each other with small, wondering smiles.

"I don't think I realized how much I was missing in life until I met you." Softly, tenderly, Grant added with heartfelt urgency: "I love you, Kelli."

She felt a surge of joy spread through her. She hadn't expected him to say the words, and she was thrilled to be able to respond in kind from her heart. "I love you, too."

He sought and found her hand, squeezing it affectionately as he brought it up between them. "It's incredible, isn't it? What's happened between us?"

"Yes," she breathed.

"I never thought it was possible to fall in love like this. So deeply, and so fast."

"Neither did I." Her smile widened. "I guess I should have, though."

"Should have? Why?"

"Whirlwind romances seem to be a common theme in my family. My brother and his wife fell in love at first sight. My grandparents got married four months after they met. My parents said they were 'struck by love' on their first date. They got engaged two weeks later."

"Two weeks!"

She nodded. "They were married four weeks after that."

"Wow. That's fast."

"The amazing thing is, all the marriages have stood the test of time, and have been very happy. My dad says when he met my mom, that was it; he knew he was going to marry her. My mother always says: *When you know, you know.*"

"I like that." He brought her hand to his lips and kissed it. "What do you think? Is it a sign?"

"A sign?"

"Do you remember what you said the day we met, when you bumped into me outside that elevator?"

Kelli cast her thoughts back to that memorable night. "I hope I said ... excuse me?"

"That's what *I* said. You said: *fate.*"

She gave a little, embarrassed gasp. "I can't believe I said that out loud. But I suddenly felt as if my entire life was about to change."

"That's how I feel now. I never thought of marriage as a viable option for me. But that's because I'd never met anyone that I could imagine sharing my life with. Since I met you, I've been thinking very differently."

Kelli's heart pounded. Was he really talking about marriage in the same breath as their first admission of love? But then, she was the one who'd brought it up, by mentioning her family history.

"We have so much in common." His eyes met hers across the pillow. "I feel like we're kindred spirits."

"So do I."

He caressed her cheek, his eyes filled with emotion. "Could you imagine being happy, married to me?"

"Is that a proposal?"

"Do you want it to be?"

"I don't know," she returned softly. "This has all happened so fast. I love you. But don't you think we both need a little time, to make sure this thing between us is real and true and lasting?"

"You're right." He kissed her deeply, his hand gently caressing her, causing sparks to spiral throughout her body. Then he moved on top of her.

"But in the meantime," he whispered against her lips, "there's something else between us that is very real and true. Let's see how long we can make it last."

"I ALWAYS KNEW you were an artist at heart," Kelli remarked.

Having gotten only the barest glimpse of Grant's house the night before, she asked for a tour the next morning before breakfast.

His home was sunny, cozy, and immaculate, built in the California ranch style with rounded arches in the open doorways. She discovered he not only shared her eye for color and attention to detail but also in decor and furnishings.

When she came upon a series of watercolor landscapes hanging in the hall—lovely desert, mountain, and ocean scenes—she stopped in surprise. Every one of them was signed with his name. "Why didn't you tell me you painted? These are wonderful."

He shrugged. "They're nothing special. I did those years ago. I haven't painted since college."

"Why not? You're really good."

"Not good enough. Not half as good as you." She started to protest but he silenced her with a kiss. "Besides, I'm too slow. What you could paint in an hour would take me half a day." The kissing went on several minutes longer before the tour guide reluctantly agreed to proceed.

"I don't believe this," Kelli said moments later, noticing a framed print hanging in the living room. "I have the same print at home."

They laughed with amazement when she opened his kitchen cabinet to set the table for breakfast and discovered they had the exact same set of stoneware dishes.

"We have similar taste in so many things, it's uncanny," Kelli commented. "I think we agree on everything except cars."

He turned from the stove where he was flipping pancakes onto plates and looked at her. He seemed to be hiding a grin. "I told you: we're kindred spirits."

She studied a casserole dish and teapot in the cabinet.

"You have the last two serving pieces I'm missing. If I moved in, we'd have sixteen of everything, and a perfect matched set."

Her cheeks grew warm as soon as she spoke the words. He hadn't brought up the idea of marriage again since their conversation the night before. And she hadn't meant to imply that they should live together.

Grant's hands slipped around her waist. "If you moved in, huh?" His breath was a moist vapor against her ear. "That's a great idea. It would be the perfect way to find out if we're meant for each other."

In his embrace, she began to melt like jelly. "Grant. My work is in Seattle."

"It doesn't have to be. Come work for me."

It was hard to concentrate when he held her this way. "I don't know ...."

"The night we met I offered you a job as creative director. I figured I could use two people in that position. Since Andy left, the spot's wide open. I don't want anyone else but you."

Flattered but uncertain, Kelli tried to organize her thoughts as she gazed up at him. "I have to admit, when I turned down your original offer, I wondered if I'd made the right decision."

"Did you?" He seemed pleased.

"I think I'd enjoy working for you. It would be exciting to live in San Francisco. But—"

"But?"

She stepped back out of his arms. "There's a lot to consider. We've only known each other for two weeks! This would mean changing my entire life. I worked hard to build up my own business. I don't know if I'm ready to give it up yet."

"Why? Are you determined to work freelance so you can prove yourself in some way? Because that's nonsense. You have nothing to prove. You're one of the most talented artists I've ever met. Any agency would be lucky to have you."

"Thanks. But it's not just about proving myself. I get a lot of satisfaction from knowing that the clients are mine—all mine—and that the creative decisions I make won't be overruled by upper management."

"Upper management? Meaning me."

"I didn't mean ...." She broke off, suddenly self-conscious. Upper management *was* Grant.

"I understand how you feel. I like being the boss. But has it really been like that, with us? To be honest, all this time, I never felt as if you were working *for* me. You were working *with* me. We make a great team."

"I felt the same way ... most of the time."

"Most of the time?" he repeated with a sigh. "Okay, I admit, I'm not perfect. But I have only the greatest respect for you and your work. And I'm trying."

"Wouldn't our relationship pose a problem at your office?"

He shrugged. "Lots of couples work together."

"But if I move down here to work for you, and things don't work out between us the way we hope ... I'd be out of a job and have to start all over."

"There is that risk," he admitted, "but I don't see that happening." He wrapped his arms around her again, heart-felt affection shining in his blue eyes.

"I love you, Kelli. The past two weeks have been the best of my life. I think we'd be good for each other. I realize this is a big decision for you. If you need time to think it through, I totally get it."

"Do you?"

"Yes. There's no rush." Teasing, he added, "Take all the time you need. One hour. Two."

Her laugh was cut off by the warm pressure of his mouth. She closed her eyes, molding her softness against his strength, thinking how perfectly they fit together, how good it could be between them.

She loved him. She wanted him. But family history or no, was it wise to live with a man she'd known for such a short time? And if she took the job, was it wise to live with —or marry—a man she worked for?

GRANT'S OFFICE opened at nine. He took her on a complete tour that morning and introduced her to his large staff.

It was an impressive setup, complete with a state-of-the-art audiovisual room that resembled a small theater. Everyone, from public relations and media placement to the clerical staff, seemed to have heard about the way Kelli had rescued The Harrington Company account, and they greeted her warmly.

The morning sped by as Kelli worked on the remaining comps for the Cassera's proposal.

Grant was so busy he only had a chance to stop in once, but she enjoyed working in the sunny, cheerful graphic art department. She joined in the bantering that flew back and forth across the room and laughed with the staff over deli sandwiches on their lunch break. Even with people from different departments rushing in and out, small erupting crises, and the usual complaints, Kelli found it a pleasant place to work.

At one o'clock, Jim poked his head in the doorway. "How's it going?"

"Great. In fact, I'm all done."

"That's terrific. Now you can join us."

"Join you where?"

"A bunch of us put in so much overtime the past week, Grant gave us the rest of the day off. We're going to Golden Gate Park to catch the exhibit on Chinese art. I hear they've got some incredible murals. Want to come?"

Kelli had never been to Golden Gate Park. The exhibit sounded tempting and going out with the group would be fun. But having seen so little of Grant today, she decided she'd rather be here when he was through. Shaking her head regretfully, she explained why she couldn't go.

"Maybe next time," Jim responded.

Kelli was cleaning up her work area, wishing she could have seen the Chinese murals, when she remembered something Ted Lazar had mentioned at their meeting at Cassera's:

I'd like to spruce up the hotel lobby if I could, but so far no one's come up with anything.

An idea popped into her head. A sudden vision for a mural on the hotel lobby's back wall. But not just any mural; a highly specialized mural ....

She got out the materials she needed and started to

work. It would take four separate paintings to show the full effect.

An hour later the first watercolor was completed. It was an exciting concept, and she couldn't wait to show it to Grant. She was about to begin on the second painting when Grant's voice resonated from the doorway.

"Kelli." He gestured with his head for her to come with him. He strode purposefully down the hall. The moment they entered his office, he shut the door, wrapped her in his embrace, and kissed her deeply.

"It's torture," he murmured, "walking past that doorway, knowing I can't just walk in and take you in my arms the way I did up at Tahoe."

"It's been tough on me, too. I kept hoping you'd come by. What have you been up to?"

"Meetings with clients. Putting out fires. The usual." He rocked her slowly back and forth in his arms. "Forget your freelance business, Kelli. Forget this place. There are too many people around. Let's open up a two-man shop. Correction. One-man one-woman shop."

She laughed. "Is that yet another new proposition, Mr. Pembroke?"

"It's a subject that should definitely come under consideration." His lips found hers again. "How are you doing on the comps?"

"Done."

"Done? You're amazing."

"I know," she quipped. "I'm working on something else now to surprise you."

"Oh? Well, finish it fast. I plan to knock off early tonight. I want to take you out on the town. Have you seen the view from Coit Tower? Been to Ghirardelli Square after dark? Ridden the glass elevator to the top of the Fairmont? Had dinner at the Blue Fox?"

She shook her head no to each question. "I was only here once, for a few days. Seventeen years ago."

He whistled. "Then you haven't really seen San Francisco. Pier 39 didn't even exist back then. We'll do it right. Tonight. Okay?"

She nodded happily. "I'd love to."

A buzzing sound interrupted them. Grant swore under his breath and picked up his phone. "Yes?" He heaved a sigh and shrugged at her apologetically. "Okay, put him on."

Grant leaned back against his desk, his tone changing to warm cordiality as he greeted the person on the other end of the line. After a short conversation, he said he'd be there at two-thirty, and bring Carl and Marc with him.

"I'm sorry," he told Kelli after he hung up, "but I have to go. Another fire to put out. I'll try to be back by four, so we can get to Coit Tower before dark." He kissed her again, lingering a long moment before pulling back. "Remember where we left off, okay?" He touched a finger to her lips.

"I will."

He walked her back to the art department. At her drafting table, he studied the watercolor she'd been working on. "What's this?"

"It's an idea I had for Cassera's lobby. A fifty-foot mural, to go with their European and Alpine theme."

"A mural?"

She reminded him of Ted's comment about the bare walls. The panorama she'd painted showed cities and towns below the snowy Alps, with flags of the seven countries whose borders they crossed. "What makes this special is the lighting system I had in mind. It changes with the time of day. And here's how it would look."

The painting showed the scene at sunrise, awash with an amber glow. "I want to do three more paintings: one at midday with a bright-blue sky, one at sunset, and a midnight sky filled with stars. We could use a black light that makes the mountains glow in the dark and mount tiny lights in the—" She saw his dubious expression and broke off. "You don't like it?"

"It's a nice idea, but a mural in the hotel lobby? That's not our territory. Why waste your time on it?"

Crestfallen, she said, "It may not be our territory now, but if we win the account, it *could* be. I thought Ted might like it. And that every little bit of creative thinking would help."

"It's creative all right." He frowned and headed for the door. "But we've got a new logo, racks of collateral materials, and two ad campaigns. That's a lot to lay on a client all at once. I don't want to confuse the issue by crossing over into interior design. Let's just present what we've got tomorrow and leave it at that. Okay?"

～

"Excuse me."

A half hour had passed. A worried Charlene stood in the doorway, looking from one graphic artist to the other, as if unsure whom to address.

Kelli had been working on the second watercolor for the Alpine scene. She was disappointed by Grant's reaction, but she liked the idea too much to throw it away. She had nothing else to do, and figured if they won the account, Grant could present the idea to Ted at some later date.

"What's wrong, Charlene?" someone asked.

"I've got Pace Printers on the line. They have a problem, but everyone who handles this is gone for the day. It's Marc's account, but he's with Grant, and they're somewhere in transit."

"Don't look at me," intoned Doug, the production artist at the table next to Kelli. "I don't get involved in that stuff."

"I'll take it." Kelli picked up the line at a nearby desk. Grant had offered her a job here as creative director, after all. She had experience with printing houses. The least she could do was try to assist in a crisis. "This is Kelli Harrison. How can I help?"

The printer explained that he had invitations on the press for one of their clients, a travel agency. A question had come up, so he was holding up the printing. Could she come down and take a look at it?

The print shop was within walking distance. Sure, Kelli told him. When she hung up, Doug frowned at her and shook his head.

"Grant only lets Dave and Jim approve press runs."

"But Dave's sick, and Jim isn't here," Kelli pointed out. "They can't hold the presses forever."

Kelli was glad to get outside and smiled to herself as she walked through the busy neighborhood to the print shop. The sky was blue, the air was crisp, and the quaint shops she passed beckoned her to come inside.

The print shop itself looked small from the outside, but

opened into a large, spotlessly clean back room where presses roared at a fever pitch.

"We followed the artwork exactly," the printer explained, leading her to one of the presses at the back. "But we think you should have asked for a lighter screen."

He picked up a sheet off the printed stack next to the press and Kelli studied it. The invitations had been designed to resemble a passport, with the travel agency's logo screened as a background pattern under the copy. A nice design, Kelli thought, although the background was a little heavy, making the copy a bit hard to read.

"See the problem?" he asked.

She nodded. "What's the deadline on these?"

"They're due at the mailing house tomorrow morning. It's critical that they get sent out on time, I was told, since they're invites to some important bash."

"If we take these off the press, how long would it take to make plates with a new screen?"

"A couple of hours. The thing is, we shut down in an hour, and this stock has to dry overnight before it can be folded. If I run this now, we can have it folded and stapled and out first thing in the morning. If I take it off, I can't print until tomorrow, and we have to wait another whole day before I fold it. The deadline will be toast."

Kelli studied the printed sheet one more time. The invitations looked beautiful. The text was readable, even if the art wasn't as perfectly designed as she might have wished. The deadline was more important, she decided, than absolute perfection.

"Roll the presses," she told the printer. To her satisfaction he grinned in delight.

She hurried back to the office, daydreaming about her upcoming night on the town with Grant. She was back at her drafting table working on her watercolor a while later when she heard a commotion. Going to the head of the stairs, she saw Grant and Marc heading up in mi-argument.

"Don't waste your time getting a client excited about something he can't have," Grant fumed. "We agreed on radio. There's no way his budget will stretch to TV. He'd waste a bundle just on the storyboards and we'd have to scrap the project in the end."

"Got it," Marc said.

When they reached the top landing, Grant turned to her.

"Kelli, what's this I hear about the invitations for Dreyfus Travel? You went down to Pace and did a press check?" His blue eyes flashed warily as if she were a stranger, someone not to be trusted.

"Yes," she said, taken aback momentarily, having expected a far different reception from him. "They called, and there was no one else to—"

"What'd you tell them?" Marc asked.

"I told them go ahead."

"Did you bring samples?" Grant asked. At her nod, he added, "Let me see one."

Back in the art department, she handed them each a printed sheet. To her dismay Grant let out a low curse. "You approved *this?*"

"I did," Kelli replied, terrified that she'd made some horrible blunder.

"It's too hard to read. The client will never go for this."

She tried to defend her decision, explaining about the deadline, but Grant kept shaking his head in disgust.

"I think it looks okay," Marc put in. "I promised they'd be mailed out tomorrow. If she hadn't approved it, we would have lost a whole day. And it wasn't Pace's fault that—"

"If Pace was worth their salt," Grant insisted, "when they recognized the issue, they would have offered to make new negs and plates and worked overtime to run the thing tonight. We still could have made the deadline. If *I'd* been there, if Jim had been there, *we* would have insisted on that and made it happen."

He turned to Kelli. "You may not have the same standards with your freelance business, but we have a reputation to maintain here. We'll be lucky if the client doesn't refuse to pay for this job."

Kelli's cheeks burned. "I'm sorry." She was determined to maintain some level of dignity in front of Marc and the other graphic artists in the room. "I was only trying to help."

"That kind of help I don't need." Grant noticed the second watercolor she'd been working on. "What are you doing? I told you not to waste your time on this!"

"I know, but I decided—"

"*You* decided?" he said tightly. "You don't make the decisions around here, Kelli. You don't work here yet."

She stared at him in disbelief. Only a few hours before, he had told her he loved her. He'd wanted her to not only move in with him but take over as his creative director. They worked so well together he'd said. They made a great team.

But could they ever really be a team?

It was fine when she'd helped him out of the jam with The Harrington Company. There, she realized, she had just followed instructions, drawn illustrations to order.

The first time she'd made a decision on her own, however, and dabbled with a creative idea without his input, he couldn't handle it.

"You're right, Grant." She faced him defiantly in the silent room. "I don't work here yet. And I never will."

CHAPTER 11

Kelli pulled into the parking lot at Cassera's Hotel and Casino the next morning and killed her car's engine.

Nothing could erase the anguish she'd felt ever since the previous afternoon when she'd stormed out of Grant's office, ignoring his calls for her to wait, calmly stating that she'd see him in Tahoe for the presentation.

It was over between them. There was no doubt in her mind about that.

It wasn't because Grant had humiliated her in front of his staff. She knew he'd arrived in a fit of temper after his argument with Marc, and his anger had snowballed. She could forgive him for that. But it didn't change the ultimate problem.

Her decision on the printing had been sound, even if he hadn't agreed. Her idea for the mural was innovative, but he hadn't been able to accept it. No matter how many times Grant claimed he'd allow her the freedom to be creative, to make her own decisions, in truth he needed to be the boss, doing things his own way.

Even though she loved him, Kelli couldn't work with him on those terms. She certainly couldn't consider spending her life with him on those terms. She'd already suffered through one disastrous relationship with a controlling man. She couldn't, *wouldn't* go through that again.

At ten o'clock sharp she entered Ted Lazar's office. Grant jumped up from his chair next to the huge desk and took her hand with a warm greeting. He looked exhausted, yet his eyes told her how sorry he was.

Kelli pasted on a brittle smile, struggling to remind herself not to think, not to feel. She had to end this now. The minute the meeting was over, she'd walk away.

Grant sat beside her, presenting the materials they'd conceived to the small, assembled group of executives and board members, explaining their ideas for the collateral materials and the ads.

During the entire meeting, she was acutely conscious of his nearness, the deep timbre of his voice, and the silent, private messages of apology he directed at her every time he turned her way. It was all she could do to maintain her composure, to make the appropriate responses when Ted asked her a question, to play the role of Grant's knowledgeable, platonic business associate, when deep inside she felt a gnawing, ever-present ache over the finality of the special and intimate relationship they had shared.

"One more thing," Grant told the group, just when she was certain they were finished, and she could make her escape. He pulled out another stack of covered art boards from his leather case.

"Kelli came up with a unique and imaginative interior design suggestion. Although it doesn't fall within the scope of this work, I present it to you as a sideline, something you might consider for the future."

She looked at him in astonishment as he uncovered four watercolors depicting the Alpine mural she had envisioned.

Four Watercolors. She'd only finished one and had barely begun the second. But there they were: all four scenes. She immediately recognized the artist's technique on the last three paintings. It matched the style of the landscapes she'd seen hanging in the hall of Grant's house. Sometime between yesterday afternoon before and this morning, he'd painted them himself.

She remembered his words: "I'm too slow. What you could paint in an hour would take me half a day." Her heart twisted at the thought of the effort this must have cost him. No wonder he looked so exhausted.

But with a pang of profound regret, she realized—no matter how lovely the thought behind it—it still didn't change anything. The basic problem was still there. Sooner or later, and no doubt on a regular basis, Grant's need to control would take over again, driving a wedge between them.

"This is your concept, Kelli," Grant added with a smile. "Can you share what you had in mind?"

Kelli mustered her enthusiasm and went over her idea for the mural. Ted and most of the board responded positively to the idea.

When the meeting ended and everyone shook hands, Ted said they'd make their decision by the end of the week and let them know.

As Kelli stepped into the empty elevator with Grant, images of the night they'd met in that same elevator were all too vivid in her mind. When the doors closed, she said quietly, "You didn't have to do that. Finish the watercolors, I mean. But thank you. It was a really nice gesture."

"I didn't mean it to be a gesture. I did it because you were right. It's a terrific idea. I should have let you follow through on it in the first place. I wish I had. But for some reason—I don't know, maybe the way you kept solving problems at my company without asking me—I guess, somehow, I felt that my authority was being threatened. I know that's ridiculous, but …."

He reached out for her hand, but she shrank back. The resulting hurt on his face made her ache inside. Yet she knew better than to let him touch her. All it would take was a tender touch, a softly uttered phrase, and she'd be putty in his hands. If she let him take her in his arms, she'd be lost all over again.

"Can we go somewhere and talk?" Grant asked.

"I'd rather not."

"We need to talk this through. I'm sorry for what happened yesterday, so incredibly sorry. I lost my temper. But I didn't mean—"

"It isn't just yesterday." The elevator stopped, and he followed her into the lobby. "Yesterday opened my eyes, that's all. You once said, there's no such thing as 'too much alike.' I disagree. We both have strong personalities, and we clash."

"No, we don't. We came up with our best ideas when we worked together. We were brilliant."

"Maybe we were. But after the creative sessions ended, you had to be the one running things. There's no way you'll ever be satisfied with anything I create or any decision I make on my own. You need to be in the driver's seat."

"No, I don't. I—"

"Yes, you do." She swallowed hard. "And let's be honest: I like that seat, too." Backing away, she added brokenly, "It was wonderful while it lasted—truly wonderful. But—"

He covered the distance between them in two strides. "I love you. You said you love me."

"I do. But—"

"Then don't give up on me—on us. Give us another chance. What we have, it's so rare. You can't just walk away from it. We can work this out."

"I've been through it before, Grant." A tear trickled down her cheek. "Let's end this now, before it gets any harder to say goodbye."

KELLI STARED into the flames in the hearth, trying to think about the Christmas week to come.

Eventually, she promised herself, her time with Grant would be no more than a distant memory. Two loving weeks. A sharing between two people that wasn't meant to last. She'd forget the pain sooner or later. She *would*.

If only she could forget now.

Over the past week, she had turned her brother's Lake Tahoe retreat into a beehive of activity. She'd had snow cleared away from around the house and the back porch and had all the windows washed. Carpet and hardwood floors had been laid in record time, and bathroom accessories had been installed. On Kyle's instructions, truckloads of furniture, bedding, kitchen supplies, and other household necessities had been delivered, all brand-new and labeled according to room.

Kelli had overseen the placement of the furniture, unpacked some of the boxes, and bought a few odds and ends to make the house more comfortable.

Now, absently fingering the texture of the new cotton sofa in the living room, Kelli felt fresh tears brim in her eyes. She may have stayed busy every day for the past week, but the nights had stretched long and lonely.

The house with its gleaming floors, lush carpet, and new furnishings seemed strange and unfamiliar. Thank goodness Kyle and his family were due to arrive any minute. Once surrounded by their love, laughter, and warmth, Kelli was certain she'd feel better.

She heard a car coming up the drive, and then the honk of a horn. Jumping up, Kelli dried her eyes and ran to the door.

It was dark, well past dinnertime, but in the warm glow from the porch light she could see a shiny silver station wagon parked next to her Rover in front of the garage. Kyle got out first and she raced down the steps, flew into her brother's arms.

"Am I glad to see you!" Kelli cried as he encased her in a hug. "How was the drive?"

"Long," he replied with a laugh. "Next time I think we'll fly."

She glanced up at Kyle, thinking, with a fresh stab of loneliness, how much like Grant he was. Not as tall, but equally as handsome, with the same rugged strength in his arms and shoulders, the same well-proportioned physique, the same dark brown hair and bright sparkle in his green eyes.

"Hey." Kyle eyed her with concern. "Is something wrong?"

"No," she lied. "Everything's fine." Brightly, to distract him, she added, "You got a new car!"

"Shows how long it's been since *you've* been down south. We bought this wagon a year ago. A few months of dragging baby paraphernalia around in the Maserati, and we'd had it."

"Do I get a hug or is this reunion reserved for siblings?" intoned a familiar, husky, feminine voice.

Kelli turned and joined in Desiree's friendly laugh as they embraced each other. Her sister-in-law's long, honey-brown hair fell in waves around her shoulders, and her amber eyes were filled with affection.

"Did you get shorter, or have I grown since I saw you last?" Kelli teased, borrowing the line her father used every time Kyle's petite wife came to visit.

"Oh, stop!" Desiree smiled. A loud wail came from inside the car, and she threw open the back door. "Didn't mean to ignore *you,* sweetie. Come see Aunt Kelli." Desiree fiddled with the child's car seat and brought out a squirming baby in overalls.

"Hi, sweetheart." Kelli took the tiny girl into her arms. "Did you have a nice trip?"

The infant stared at her solemnly, her pale, sweet face

surrounded by wisps of soft, light brown hair. Kelli couldn't believe how much she'd grown. "I missed you, Denise."

"That's Daniella," Desiree corrected.

"I did it again!" Kelli smiled and kissed the baby's chubby cheek. "Someday I'll learn to tell you two apart."

Kyle brought over his other identical twin daughter, moving her small arm in a wave. "Say hi, Denise." The toddler broke into a silent, toothy grin.

"How old are they now?" Kelli asked.

"Fourteen months," Desiree answered. "Wait until you see how well they're walking. I can't keep up."

The pride in Kyle's and Desiree's faces, and the love they radiated, brought fresh moisture to Kelli's eyes.

Everything, she thought, seemed to make her cry these days.

"I'm so glad you're all here." Kelli blinked rapidly, hoping they wouldn't notice her tears as she held Daniella close, trying to concentrate on the happiness of the moment. But somehow, the happiness seemed shallow and incomplete.

THEY SPENT the evening combing through the house. Kelli shared anecdotes about the work that had been done. As she'd expected, Kyle, the perfectionist, made a list of things that needed to be finished or fixed, but overall, he and Desiree were delighted with the results.

"Thank you *so* much," they both exclaimed over and over.

"If you ever get tired of advertising, you can start a whole new profession as a contractor," Kyle insisted. "Or an interior designer. You did a terrific job, and I'll always be grateful."

They also appreciated all the unpacking Kelli had done on their behalf and promised to reimburse her for everything she'd bought for the place.

When they reached the garage, where she'd moved Grant's graphics furniture and supplies, Kyle reacted with surprise. "I figured Grant would have cleared all this stuff out by now."

"I haven't heard from him in a while," she replied quickly. "I thought I'd ship it back to his agency next week."

Kyle looked at her curiously. She had told him earlier that the advertising project went well. "Why haven't you heard from him? What happened between you two?"

"Nothing. We were just business partners for a couple of weeks, that's all. He's probably been too busy to—"

"Just business partners?" he cut in skeptically. "That's not the impression I got when you called after the storm. I recall a distinct ... lilt to your voice. A sort of ringing happiness. And something about making good use of the time."

To her frustration, Kelli felt herself blush. "Well, we did become ... close for a while. But it didn't work out." She took a deep breath. "To tell you the truth, I'd rather not talk about it."

Kyle nodded, and didn't bring up the subject again.

The next afternoon, they all piled into the station wagon and went out to buy a Christmas tree. Later, they set up the fragrant, nine-foot pine in the living room.

"Wait," Kyle told Desiree, when she started unloading a

box. "I brought *my* Christmas ornaments. Isn't it my turn to decorate the tree?"

Desiree made a face. "I don't want another tree like the one two years ago."

"Kyle," Kelli interrupted, "you didn't force Desiree to live through an entire Christmas with that boring tree of yours, did you?"

"See?" Desiree unwrapped a delicate Mrs. Claus figurine. "I'm not the only one who thinks your tree is boring."

"Every single year, the tree at his condo looked exactly the same." Kelli grimaced. "All silver ornaments. Very modern. Very monotone."

"And very cold," Desiree nodded.

"A great tree for an appliance store," Kelli added.

"It's simple and clean," Kyle responded defensively. "It's not a hodgepodge, which is the only way to describe your tree." Kyle shook his head in disbelief. "Desiree's been saving ornaments since the day she was born and insists on hanging every single one on the tree."

"My ornaments are beautiful," Desiree argued.

The coffee table was strewn with an array of ornaments made out of wood, porcelain, glass, fabric, and crystal. Desiree held up a tiny, knitted, red Christmas stocking ornament.

"My great-grandmother made this. It has sentimental value. A lot of these do. I've tried to explain this to my husband, but if something's not brand new, he thinks it should be thrown away."

"I do not," Kyle protested. "I like silver ornaments because they're bright and shiny. All these other things don't stand out. They just look dull and brown, the same color as the tree. And *that's* monotone to me."

Desiree's face fell. Kelli felt the same pang of sudden understanding and compassion. She knew that Kyle was color blind, but she'd forgotten, for the moment, that a fresh green Christmas tree, covered in red and green ornaments, must look very different to him.

"I think," Kelli said after a beat, "what you should do is compromise."

"Compromise?" Kyle repeated.

She suggested that they use half of Kyle's silver ornaments and half of Desiree's. And that they rotate in the unused ones every other year.

"That could work." Desiree eyed her husband fondly. "What do you say, sweetheart? Shall we compromise?"

Kyle's lips twitched, then spread into a grin. "Who could say no in the face of such wisdom?"

When the tree was finished, they all stood back in admiration.

"It's the prettiest tree we've ever had," Desiree announced.

Kyle kissed her. "I think compromising has its advantages."

The next kiss lasted a long time. Kelli had to look away, suddenly feeling in the way and more than a little envious of their closeness.

Grabbing her parka from the hall closet, Kelli quietly let herself out the front door.

She'd wanted to hike along the beach, but it was covered with snow and she wasn't wearing boots, so she headed down the driveway instead and followed the road as it curved down past the lake into the trees.

The afternoon sun felt warm on her face. The sky was blue and the tall pines were lightly dusted with snow. But the scene held no beauty for her today.

How was she going to get through an entire week, Kelli wondered, living in the same house with Kyle and Desiree? Every look, every word that passed between them—even during an argument—showed how much they loved and needed each other.

She had tried to deny it to herself for the past eight days, but she could no longer ignore it: she missed Grant with an ache so fierce that it threatened to tear her apart.

Kelli wondered what he was he was doing at that moment. It was Saturday. Was he alone at the office, getting caught up on his work? Or at home in his sunny, cheerful kitchen, fixing a late lunch on the set of stoneware dishes that matched her own?

The memory of their morning there together came flooding back. Once again she could feel the warmth of his arms around her, could see the glow of affection in his eyes as he'd said, *"I love you. The past two weeks have been the best of my life. I think we'd be good for each other."*

Before she met Grant, she'd considered herself a happy person. She had looked forward to exploring her independence and to operating her small business in Seattle. But since he came into her life, everything had changed.

She loved him.

She wanted him.

She needed him.

But how, she asked herself, could they resolve the

conflicts that constantly cropped up between them? What did you do when two people both always wanted to have their own way?

Suddenly she saw Kyle and Desiree arguing over the Christmas tree, and heard herself saying, *What you should do is compromise.*

Kelli's heart quickened. The answer had been there all the time. She'd been so caught up in her need to be strong and self-sufficient that she'd missed the point of what love and life and creative endeavors were all about.

Compromise.

Grant had compromised often and willingly over their work. Every time they'd put their heads together and combined the best ideas of each, they'd achieved a far better result than either could have accomplished on their own. In some areas he was more knowledgeable than she was. In others he could learn from her.

What if Grant had kowtowed to her every thought and wish? What kind of a partner would he have made? Yes, his instinct was to control things. But she was lucky to have found a man who asserted his own opinions, yet was confident enough to know when to give in.

He'd apologized for panning her idea about the mural and had gone far beyond the call of duty to prove he respected her ideas. With Grant, she might not get unqualified approval all the time, but she knew she'd get help and unqualified affection.

Yes, yes, she thought, as she turned and raced back up the road. *We can work it out. We can.*

She'd get in her car, zip back to San Francisco, and tell him how she felt. Better yet, she'd get on the phone and call him this minute. She'd tell him she loved him and wanted to spend the rest of her life with him.

It seemed to take forever to get home. She hadn't realized she'd walked so far. When at last, panting for breath, she caught sight of the house, a new thought struck her. She'd been so adamant that it was over the last time she saw Grant. She couldn't forget the disappointment and anger in his eyes. What if he wasn't willing to risk being hurt again? What if he couldn't forgive her for walking away?

Please, Grant, she thought, her heart pounding as she ran. *You were so right. We are good for each other. You have to still care.*

Instead of following the road all the way up to the driveway, she took a shortcut across the snowy embankment. Her shoes were soaked through by the time she hurried up the steps to the back porch. She paused outside the sliding glass door, catching her breath and stomping the snow off her shoes. One hand on the door handle, she glanced inside.

Kyle was laughing. Desiree sat cross-legged on the floor, playing with Denise—or was it Daniella? A man stood next to her, holding the other twin in his arms.

It was Grant!

He said something that made the little girl clap her hands with delight.

Kelli's joy on seeing him was so great, she couldn't move. She watched him for a moment through the glass, wondering what she should say now that he was actually here.

He looked up, and his gaze met hers through the window. His smile vanished.

Kelli's heart seemed to lurch to a stop. She could read no message in his eyes. Her worst fears seemed to be confirmed: he was still angry. He hadn't forgiven her. Then why had he come?

With a stab of intense disappointment, she guessed the answer: he was here to pick up the graphics supplies and equipment from the garage, that's all.

Don't give up, she told herself. *Somehow, you have to get him to listen.* Taking a deep breath to steady herself, Kelli slid open the door.

"There she is!" Kyle announced jovially. "We were going to send a search party if you didn't show up soon."

"We've been entertaining your friend," Desiree explained. "Or should I say, he's been entertaining *us*. We just heard how you saved an account for him with that faster-than-lightning drawing arm of yours." She laughed, but Grant didn't join in.

Kelli met Grant's gaze across the room. A long moment passed, the most uncomfortable of her life. What should she say? Do?

Kyle broke the silence. "Well, I guess you two have a lot to talk about. We'll just go upstairs."

He caught Desiree's eye. She stood quickly, cradling the baby in her arms. "Yes. It's time for the girls' nap."

"Come on, Daniella." Kyle lifted the other little girl from Grant's arms and kissed her cheek.

"It's all right," Grant said. "You two don't have to leave. We'll go outside." He glanced at Kelli and added politely, "That is, if you don't mind."

"Of course not." Kelli's voice didn't sound like her own. She backed out onto the porch and Grant followed. Sliding the door closed, he crossed the redwood decking to the far side. She stood a few feet away, nervously clutching the rail, unsure how to begin.

"The house looks great," he said finally. "You must have really worked hard to get so much done in a week."

She shrugged uncertainly. "I didn't have anything else to do." When he didn't say more, she lowered her eyes. "I guess you came to clear out the studio?"

"No, I didn't."

"Oh." She felt a small burst of hope, but still couldn't look at him.

After a long pause, he said softly, "I missed you."

Her eyes flew up to meet his, and she took a sharp breath. "I missed you, too. So much." *Now*, she told herself. *Tell him now.* "Grant," she began, "I've been thinking all week about—"

"Wait. Don't say anything, not until I've had my chance." He shoved his hands in his pockets. "I've rehearsed this speech about fifty times. Let me get it out there."

He took a deep breath and went on. "I'm sorry for what I said at the office that day. It was inexcusable. I just hope you can forgive me. This past week has been hell. I've been alone a long time. I thought I was fine. But I realize now I'd just accepted loneliness as a fact of life. You're all I think about. You said we're so much alike that we clash, but I don't buy it. All the things we have in common are a gift.

"We may have stepped on each other's toes a few times, but we're learning. We both want the same things out of life—to use our creative instincts, to build something from nothing, to do the best job we can. But what's the point of doing great work if you have no one to love, no one to share it with? We've got something special together. You know we do."

Kelli felt a surge of joy. "I agree."

"You do?" He looked surprised, yet afraid to hope. "Then why'd you run out on me? I want you to have equal say in everything we do. If you don't want to work for me, fine. Run your own business. But can you do it in San Francisco? I'll give you some of my clients to get started, good accounts. I know they'll be well taken care of."

"You would do that?"

"Of course, I would. But that's just a small part of this. I'm talking about our *lives* here. I realize this has happened incredibly fast. But your mom had it right: *When you know, you know.* I think *I've* known since the moment I bumped into you outside that elevator. Why do you think I proposed that unorthodox working arrangement? I had to find out if there was any future for us. And there *is*. I want to make a home together, a life together, have children together." He paused, his voice deep and his eyes brimming with emotion. "Kelli, I love you. Will you marry me?"

Happiness bubbled up inside her. Could he see, in her own expression, the depth of love that lit her heart? "Yes."

"Yes?" he repeated, unable to hide his delight.

"Yes. Yes! I love you. I'll marry you!" She couldn't contain her joy any longer and threw her arms around his neck. "If you'd given me half a chance, I was just about to ask you."

His arms tightened around her and she both felt and heard his answering laugh.

"I had six more arguments prepared. I thought it might take weeks to persuade you. What made you change your mind?"

"Somewhere along the line, I learned the value of compromise."

"Ah, yes. Compromise. I think we'll be doing a lot of that. And be better off for it, too." His kiss was sweet and tender. "You know, I never got my night on the town in San Francisco."

"There'll be time for plenty of nights on the town now."

"Should we go in and tell Kyle and Desiree? They must be dying to know what's going on."

"Not yet." He took her hand. "Come with me. I have something to show you."

He led her around to the front of the house. She stopped short when she saw the car parked next to hers in the driveway.

"I don't believe it!" She ran to take a closer look. It was an old Rover, the identical model to hers, the same exact shade of British racing green. Except that *this* car had been perfectly restored. It had a sparkling new paint job, the imitation wood inside had been replaced by real burl wood, and the seats were covered with luxurious doeskin.

"Oh!" She looked in the window breathlessly. "It's beautiful! When did you get it?"

"About five years ago."

She stared at him. "Five years ago? But then why …."

She thought back to the night they'd met, remembering his astonishment when he first saw her car. She'd thought he was making fun of her eclectic taste. She realized now that he'd simply been surprised by the coincidence.

She remembered, too, how she'd defended her old car with fierce pride. No wonder he hadn't said anything about *his* Rover. Her car looked like an old clunker compared to his. He hadn't wanted to embarrass her or destroy her illusions.

"I guess I was pretty snooty about the whole thing, wasn't I?" She sighed. "I'm surprised you didn't put me in my place on the spot."

"I admired your pride. A good Rover fanatic is hard to find."

"Yours is a masterpiece. How am I ever going to get into my car after this?"

"There's nothing wrong with your car that a little money can't fix."

"You mean we can restore it like yours?"

"Anything you want."

She hugged him. "This is great! I can't wait. Just one more thing we'll have a matched set of." He laughed, hugging her back, and she added, "*Now* I see how you knew which part to get for my car. But how did you get it so fast?"

"I had an extra one on hand, just in case of emergency."

"Good advance planning."

He grinned. "So. Are you going to start your own agency, or come work with me?"

"As creative director?"

"No, as a full partner."

Her eyes widened in astonishment. She could see that he meant it. "I'll take it."

"I'm glad." He kissed her and she responded, wanting to pour into him all the love and happiness she felt.

"There's only one little problem on the horizon," she murmured, "that we'll have to discuss someday."

"What's that?"

"You want four children. I want two."

"A definite impasse."

"What should we do about it?"

"Compromise."

"Three?"

He nodded.

"It's a deal." She kissed him again to seal the bargain. "I predict a good sixty or seventy years of wedded bliss ahead of us."

"The sky's the limit."

She caught her breath. "I almost forgot to ask! Did we win the Cassera's account, or not?"

His eyes sparkled and he couldn't stop a wide smile. "What do you think?"

She gasped with delight and he lifted her off the ground, spinning her in a circle, their joyous exclamations echoing above the treetops.

Please leave a review for TWO WEEK DEAL!

Reader reviews are so appreciated! They can be short or long, or even just a star rating. Reviews are such a big help to an author.

Thank you so much!

Join Syrie's newsletter mailing list at www.syriejames.com to receive the latest news about upcoming releases and special offers just for subscribers!

I have a special place in my heart for whirlwind romances —an immediate attraction between two people that rapidly turns to love. Maybe it's because my husband and I fell in love the night we met.

Or maybe it's because my family (going back four generations that I know of!) has had many examples of couples who met, fell in love, and married within a matter of weeks or months. All these marriages have stood the test of time and have been very happy.

It was such a thrill to give this same family history to Kelli!

Two Week Deal is one of the first books I ever wrote. It was originally published under the title *The Sky's the Limit,* and later as *Propositions.* Writing it—and revising it for this new edition—was a great joy for me. And it's a personal story, for oh-so-many reasons.

I worked in advertising for several years as a graphic artist and I enjoyed the dynamics of that inventive field. I spent many a winter skiing the slopes at Lake Tahoe and consider it one of the most beautiful places on earth.

Like Grant, in my youth, my friends and I used to wander through the casinos at South Lake Tahoe as fascinated onlookers. Although I'm of Kelli's mind—I don't have the nerve to gamble—I still find the atmosphere of a casino exciting.

I love that this book is set in the '80s, at a simpler time before cell phones, computers, and the internet changed the way we do everything. The world of graphic arts and design is completely different now. But the basics of the creative process remain the same. So do the joys we experience in a new relationship, on the road to falling in love.

Love at first sight may be rare, but I know from personal experience that it's possible. As one of my characters says in this novel, *When you know, you know.*

ACKNOWLEDGMENTS

Many thanks to Eric Fütterer for his insight regarding South Lake Tahoe, the casino industry, and the classic Rover automobile. Huge thanks to Paula Fisher Thompson for her contributions in the advertising arena.

Thank you to my wonderful agent, Tamar Rydzinski, for her endless support, advice, and encouragement.

A heart full of gratitude to my dear husband Bill, my soul mate and kindred spirit, for all the love and a lifetime of cherished memories. I miss you with every breath I take.

And as always, to my readers. Thank you for your enthusiasm about my books and for sharing them with your friends and book clubs. I am so thankful for every one of you!

Read on for an excerpt from

NOCTURNE

by Syrie James

A haunting story of forbidden love

PRAISE FOR NOCTURNE:

• *Best Snowbound Romance Novel Bookbub*

• *Best Novel of The Year Suspense Magazine*

• *Best Novel of The Year Romance Reviews*

• *Favorite Novel of The Year Austenesque Reviews*

"The kind of book that makes you want to turn off the phone and the television so you can do nothing but read."

—*Barnes & Noble Romantic Read of the Week*

NOCTURNE - EXCERPT

CHAPTER ONE

IT BEGAN SNOWING AT NINE. Delicate flakes were still sifting down two hours later as Nicole Whitcomb reluctantly loaded her carry-on suitcase and small backpack into her rental car and slammed the trunk.

She took one last second to appreciate the hushed descent of the gentle white flakes against the iron gray sky and to drink in the picturesque view of the snow-capped hotel against the backdrop of the ski slopes and surrounding forest.

I wish I could live here, Nicole thought for the hundredth time, as she inhaled deeply the crisp, pine-scented mountain air.

She hated to leave all this beauty to go back to the city, and to the stress and tedium of her job. After brushing off the accumulation of snow from her front and back windshields, she unlocked the car, slipped behind the wheel, knocked the snow off her fur-lined boots, and started the engine.

Nicole knew she had to hurry. The weather report had

said a big storm was coming into the Steamboat Springs area. When she'd called the Denver airport, however, they said it was sunny and clear, and assured her that her flight to San Jose was departing as scheduled.

She figured it shouldn't take more than forty-five minutes up the mountain road to reach Rabbit Ears Pass, the first of several summits en route. All the roads were open, so after that it should be an easy three-hour drive to Denver.

It was cold inside the car and Nicole shivered as she turned on the windshield wipers, heater, and defroster. Leaving on her fuzzy light blue scarf and hat, she strapped on her seat belt, exited the parking lot, and drove through the quaint Steamboat Springs ski village.

There was a good two feet of snow on the ground in the uncleared areas, but so far only a light dusting on the road. Even so, as she turned onto Highway 40 and headed south, she carefully moderated her speed. It had been a while since she'd driven in these conditions.

It was her first time in Colorado, a place she'd always longed to visit—and it was as beautiful as she'd imagined it would be. She'd always loved the snow. During the years she'd lived in Seattle, it had been a hop, skip, and jump to the nearest ski area, and she couldn't count how many delightful hours she'd spent on the slopes with her friends.

Since she moved back to California three years ago, however, she'd given up all that.

At the thought of that move and the reason behind it, Nicole's stomach knotted with anxiety. The memory of that awful day and all that happened afterward still filled her with self-recrimination and doubt. Would she ever be able to forget?

Nicole frowned, shoving the thought away, determined not to let it spoil her mood. She'd just spent a wonderful long weekend with dear friends she hadn't seen in years. When her best friend, Chloe, had announced her intention to have a ski resort wedding, Nicole had laughed at first—the idea had seemed ludicrous and impractical—but in the end it had been fabulous.

The wedding had taken place high atop a ski slope at Steamboat Springs, with the bridal party in formal wear and everyone on skis. After the ceremony, most of the people had ridden the chairlift back down, but Nicole—on a dare from one of the groomsmen—had blithely skied down the mountain. It had involved tucking her long bridesmaid's dress into her thermal leggings, which Chloe had laughingly insisted was scandalous and beneath the dignity of a twenty-nine-year-old woman. But Nicole hadn't cared; she couldn't resist the challenge.

The newlyweds and most of the other guests had left after two days, but Nicole stayed one more day to go skiing on her own—and what a blast it had been! Sailing down a white mountain with the crisp air in her face always felt like heaven. She couldn't wait to show the pictures to her coworkers and to the kids at the museum and the library that weekend.

The car had warmed up now. Nicole removed her hat and gloves, glancing briefly in the rearview mirror to smooth back her long, wavy, reddish-gold hair. She'd left the town of Steamboat Springs far behind.

The snow was falling faster.

Nicole increased the speed of the windshield wipers, focusing her attention on the road. For the first time, she began to wonder if she'd made a mistake in staying the extra day. The drive back to Denver would have been so much easier yesterday, when the weather had been clear.

The road began to climb through a wooded area now. Nicole had read that the highway gained an incredible 2,500 feet in about seven miles during this stretch, as it made its way up the side of the Gore Range through Routt National Forest toward the pass. The view here should be expansive, but instead it was obscured by low, dark clouds.

Nicole felt another stab of worry as she crept along. She'd been lucky to rent a car with four-wheel drive, but it wouldn't help if she encountered black ice. Worse yet, it was becoming more and more difficult to see.

The storm had come in way faster than she'd expected. The wind howled. There had been a couple of cars behind her at the beginning, but they'd long since disappeared from view, and she'd only passed a few cars coming the other way.

Should I turn back? Nicole wondered.

She didn't want to get stuck on this road in the middle of a blizzard—but she couldn't miss her flight. She'd already been gone five days, and she'd left a ton of work on her desk. She had to relieve the neighbor taking care of her cat. She didn't want to pay for another night's lodging or go through the hassle of changing her airline ticket.

No, she decided; she'd press on. The hotel desk clerk had been confident that she'd be over the pass and out of this weather system before she knew it.

On the drive up, Nicole had made a point of looking for

the sign marking the summit of Rabbit Ears Pass at 9,426 feet, announcing the precise location of the Continental Divide—the line that ran from northwestern Canada along the crest of the Rocky Mountains all the way to Mexico, and divided the flow of water between the Pacific and Atlantic oceans.

Nicole remembered smiling when she'd caught sight of the gray rock formation on a forested peak to the north, for which the pass was named. When viewed from a certain angle, the formation did sort of resemble the ears of a rabbit. But she knew that the summit was still more than a dozen miles ahead. At the rate she was crawling, it could take almost an hour to reach it.

Nicole used the snowbank at the right side of the highway as her guide, staying just a few feet inside it. At a sharp crook in the road, she reduced her speed even further, carefully navigating around the bend. Through the swirling flakes in the air, the steep, snow-covered slope on the north side of the road was partially visible.

Suddenly a loud crack erupted from above, followed by a low hissing sound.

What on earth was that? Nicole wondered, alarmed, instinctively pressing on the accelerator and speeding forward. The hissing behind her grew louder, turning into an ominous, growing rumble.

Glancing into the rearview mirror, Nicole was shocked to see an enormous slab of snow slide off the mountainside in a great, rushing torrent and cover the entire road behind her.

An avalanche! she thought in terror. If she'd been driving any more slowly, it would have buried her.

There was no turning back now, Nicole realized, even if she'd wanted to. With her heart in her throat, she continued up the road, crawling on for what seemed like a century.

The highway soon leveled off. The harsh wind stirred up snow from the drifts below that mingled in a frenzy with the flakes falling from the sky. Snow was smacking against the windshield at such a furious rate that the wiper blades couldn't keep up. Nicole struggled to see through a gathering veil of white.

The highway was covered by at least six inches of snow now, and it was growing deeper by the minute. She had to get over the pass—and soon—before this turned into a total whiteout. She pressed harder on the gas and forged on, holding tight to the wheel.

The accident happened so quickly.

One minute, Nicole was driving along under perfect control; the next instant, the road was slipping out from under her and the car was spinning into a terrifying right-hand slide. In a panic, she jammed on the brakes and jerked the wheel to the left, even as her brain shouted, No, stupid, that's the wrong thing to do and to her horror, it only made things worse.

The car skidded and then hurled itself off the road into the embankment.

A scream tore from Nicole's throat as the entire world turned upside down. A shattering pain spiraled through her head as it slammed against something hard. There was a jarring crunch, an explosion of glass, another crunch, and then the rolling stopped, and the world righted itself again.

Nicole sat unmoving, dazed and confused, her head

pounding. She struggled to get her bearings. She was still seat-belted and sitting upright. A bitterly cold wind blew in through her shattered side windows. Her lap and the interior of the car were strewn with small, scattered fragments of glass. The windshield was still intact but heavily damaged with a spider web of cracks, and the view was obscured by snow and pine branches. From what she could make out, the car had landed beneath a tree.

Okay, she told herself. It's not as bad as it looks. You ran off the road, but you're still alive.

There were no cuts on her hands, but she felt an oozing from the left side of her throbbing temple and touched it. Her fingers came away smeared with blood.

Blood.

Panic spiraled through her and she gasped aloud, extending her hand as far as humanly possible from her face. *Blood.* She couldn't look at it. The sight made her stomach churn. The pounding in her skull increased, as the horror came flooding back.

Blood. Blood everywhere. Blood pouring onto the bed and covering the floor... She was bleeding. From the head. Stop the blood. Stop it. Now!

Glancing around frantically for her purse and a tissue, she gave up and grabbed her neck scarf instead, pressing it firmly against her forehead. What should I do? she wondered, fighting down the panic, struggling to think despite the throbbing in her head. Call 911? Woozily, she retrieved her cell phone one-handed from her coat pocket and cursed. No signal.

The faint hum of a car engine made her tense with anticipation: was someone coming?

No, she decided, disappointed; it was just her own motor idling. She snapped on her flashers but couldn't see any evidence that they were working. She tried to open her car door, but it wouldn't budge.

Peering out through her broken side window, she realized that the car had sunk so deeply into the snowbank that it was half buried. The only way to get out was through the window. But—did she want to get out? Her head was bleeding. There was no way she could dig the car out and get it back on the road.

And where would she go on foot? She was in the middle of nowhere, surrounded by a national forest. As far as she knew, no one lived here; it was all government-owned land. The road behind her was blocked by an avalanche. Who knew how many miles it was to the pass up ahead, much less to the next town?

She couldn't recall seeing any call boxes on the road, and even if she could find one, how long would she last out in the blizzard? Visibility was poor and getting worse. She wasn't sure she could properly judge distance or direction; she might walk off the road and become hopelessly lost.

Better to stay in the car, she decided, and pray that someone would come along—however unlikely that might be. She gave the horn a few sharp blasts, and then leaned on it long and hard, but the sound was muffled by the roar of the wind. With a sigh, she gave up. What was the point? Who was going to hear a horn out here?

Nicole shivered. She considered leaving the engine running to keep the heater on but realized it could never keep the car warm with snow blowing in through the open windows. She turned off the ignition, leaving the key in place, knowing that it was going to get very cold, very fast.

Why did she feel so light-headed?

Still pressing the scarf against her forehead, Nicole leaned back against the seat and closed her eyes against the excruciating pain. Her thoughts drifted. She was dizzy. So dizzy.

Disconnected images flitted through her mind: the blue-green gleam of her tabby cat's eyes; the potted red Anthurium on her apartment windowsill; her friends' laughing faces over nachos and frosty margaritas; building a sandcastle on a sunny beach with her darling nieces; the giddy, gap-toothed grin of a little Native Alaskan girl.

No, Nicole thought desperately, stay awake. Stay conscious. Her last thought, as she felt her hand drop uselessly to her side, was:

Is this it? Am I going to die?

ABOUT THE AUTHOR

SYRIE JAMES is a *USA Today* and international bestselling author of more than a dozen critically acclaimed novels of historical fiction, romance, and young adult fiction that have been published in 21 languages, including *Dracula, My Love* and the #1 Amazon bestselling Victorian historical romance *Duke Darcy's Castle*.

Hailed by Los Angeles Magazine as the "queen of nineteenth century re-imaginings," Syrie loves to write about strong women and bold heroes whose chemistry is off the chart, and enjoys sending them on challenging journeys of growth and discovery.

A huge fan of All Things English, Syrie's books have

been *Library Journal* Editor's Picks of the Year (*The Lost Memoirs of Jane Austen* and *Jane Austen's First Love*), received starred reviews from *Publisher's Weekly* and *Kirkus* (ie. *The Missing Manuscript of Jane Austen*), and won numerous awards including the Audiobook Audie (*The Secret Diaries of Charlotte Brontë*).

A member of the Writer's Guild of America, Historical Novel Society, and Jane Austen Society of North America, Syrie has sold scripts to film and television and addressed organizations and literary conferences across the U.S., Canada, and in England.

Syrie's work as a playwright has been produced in New York, Los Angeles, and Montreal, and she has taken to the boards herself, appearing many times on stage as Jane Austen.

Syrie lives in Los Angeles a stone's throw from her two sons and their wives, where she enjoys long walks, flower gardens, and spends far too much time at her computer.

To learn more, please visit: **syriejames.com**.

Sign up to receive Syrie's newsletter for updates about her next release and other bookish treats!

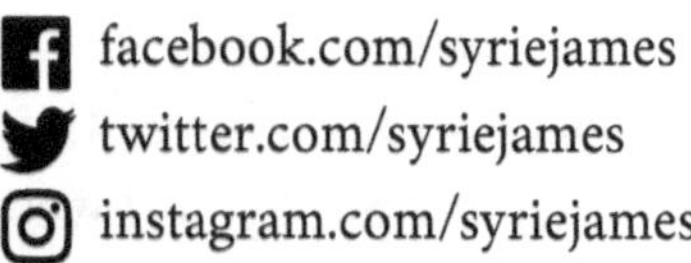

www.ingramcontent.com/pod-product-compliance
Lightning Source LLC
Chambersburg PA
CBHW021127190726

48288CB00008B/2535